COMMIT TO VIOLENCE

Praise for Roy Glenn

COMMIT TO VIOLENCE

ROY GLENN

Escapism
Entertainment

Escapism Entertainment
1038-5 Dunn Avenue
30
Jacksonville, FL 32218

ISBN-13: 978-0-615-31751-9
ISBN-10: 0-615-31751-0

First Printing: November 2009

10 9 8 7 6 5 4 3 2 1

COMMIT TO
VIOLENCE

CHAPTER ONE

Ebony Washington had the world at her feet. She was young, and she was beautiful. Ebony had a dream job which paid her enough money to get everything she ever wanted. She bought nice clothes, drove a new Volvo and she lived in a nice apartment near the Hudson River.

And Ebony was in love.

She drove her car slowly down West 132nd Street, looking for a place to park. As she drove past her apartment and turned onto Riverside Drive, she thought parking was the only thing that she regretted about living in Harlem. Even though she could now afford to live anywhere she wanted, she was born and raised in Harlem and wouldn't think of living anywhere else.

The last few days had been hard for her. It's not an easy thing to hear bad things about the one you love, but sometimes you have to—even if it's just to give you an opportunity to ask questions and give them an opportunity to respond. *It's good to clear the air sometimes,* Ebony thought. *Get things out in the open.*

She had spent the better part of the evening with Martin. They had dinner at Via Brasil on 46th street.

Ebony liked eating there. The food was excellent and the portions were always huge. She usually had the Misto, which was mixed grill skewered with Brazilian sausage, beef, chicken and pork, but that night she opted for the Frango Bossa Nova, which consisted of fried diced chicken in a garlic lemon sauce. After dinner, they went for drinks at People Lounge on Allen Street, another one of her favorite places. She liked the atmosphere, with its dark wood tables that accented the comfortable apple-green suede couches. The ample recessed lighting, the den-like atmosphere, the chocolate-brown walls, and the waterfall pane made the place feel so romantic.

Over Lychee martini's she asked Martin about the rumors she'd heard about him being involved with gangsters and ordering the execution of a man in Mexico when things didn't go the way they were planned. It made her feel a lot better when Martin looked her in the eyes and told her that those things weren't true.

Martin told her that he had heard the rumors and was doing everything in his power to put a stop to them. Then he assured her that he wasn't the type of man to be involved in anything like that. He even seemed to be a little hurt and somewhat disappointed that she would ask him questions like that. Ebony could feel the sincerity in his voice coming through loud and clear when he told her, "I love you, Ebony. I wouldn't do anything that would mess up what we have here," Martin said to her and kissed her hand. "I would do anything for you."

Anything but divorce your wife, Ebony thought.

On her way home she gave some thought to the fact that she was in love with a married man. *Hell, I'm not the first and I won't be the last,* she thought. But no matter how she tried to rationalize what she was doing, the facts were still the same—she didn't seem to care. His wife couldn't love him as much as she did. The frigid bitch could never make love to him the way she did. And he didn't love her; not anymore. He couldn't love his wife the way that he loved her. He couldn't, and that was all there was to it.

Ebony turned on Riverside Drive and circled the block again, thinking maybe she should end all the drama and look into getting a garage. She finally spotted a place to park and began the three-block walk toward her apartment.

She had walked about a block when Ebony heard footsteps coming up quickly behind her. Ebony looked over her shoulder and saw two men walking behind her. She began to walk faster, and so did her pursuers. Once she rounded the corner of 132nd Street, Ebony began to run as fast as she could in a tight skirt and heels. As the men hit the corner they began to run after her.

Two doors down from her building, Ebony fell but got up quickly. But it was too late. They were on her now. She stumbled to her stairs and fell again. She turned and looked into the face of her attacker, who stood over her with a gun pointed at her.

"No! Please don't! NO!"

CHAPTER TWO

Kenny Lucas ordered another drink and thought about the old days. He had worked for Mike Black for years. Back when somebody was trying to kill Shy, it was Kenny who provided Black with the information that put them on to James Kerns, and he was the key to it all. "The hit was set up then. But it didn't get paid for until a week or so later in Detroit."

"You get a description?" Shy asked.

"Not a good one: Black man wearin' a hat and sunglasses, about five-eight, maybe five-ten."

"That's it?" Black asked.

"There's a place in Brooklyn, a chop shop. Guy there named James Kerns is supposed to have arranged the meet with Leon." Because of that piece of information, Shy was able to find and eliminate her enemies.

After Black and Shy got married and left for the Bahamas, Freeze took over and Kenny became one of his top lieutenants.

And then Freeze died.

There were a lot of people that blamed Nick for Freeze's death. It was the night that Mylo, who turned out to be a rogue DEA agent, tried to fix the Middle

Weight Championship. When that didn't go his way, Mylo tried to get away. Nick and Freeze caught up to him, but neither Nick nor Freeze thought to take Mylo's gun.

Mylo knew that if he went anywhere with Nick and Freeze they would kill him. He reached for his gun and turned to Freeze. The move caught both Nick and Freeze off guard. Mylo fired two shots to Freeze's stomach.

The crowd ran for cover at the sound of gunfire and Mylo ran away with them. Freeze grabbed his stomach and fell into Nick's arms.

"Don't let him get away, Nick," Freeze told Nick as he laid Freeze on the ground.

"I'm not leaving you," Nick said to Freeze before he died. And even though Nick found and killed Mylo three days later, Freeze was still dead, and there were those in Black's organization that hold Nick responsible, and Kenny Lucas was one of them.

Kenny had finished his drink and was about to leave the club when Bo Freeman came and sat down next to him. Before Freeze died, Bo was his enforcer.

Freeze brought Bo in, taught him the game. Then Bo got arrested and did five years for criminal possession of stolen property, illegal possession of a vehicle identification number plate, and conspiracy. It wasn't too long after he got out that Freeze put Bo in place, running the cloning operation.

Then Nick let Freeze die.

Like a lot of people, Bo thought that when Freeze was killed that Black would tap him to takeover. And like Kenny, Bo was one of the people that thought Nick was responsible for Freeze's death.

Bo ordered a round of drinks and Kenny ordered the next two. After awhile the subject turned, as it usually did when Bo was around, to Nick.

"That and the fact that I don't think the mutha fucka is up to the job. Too busy chasin' that young pussy around to be about his job," Bo said and turned up his drink. He signed to the bartender to bring them another round.

"Sounds like you want some of that young pussy," Kenny said and finished his drink.

"The bitch got body, but all I'm sayin' is Freeze never let ho's get in the way of business."

The bartender poured another round. "True." Kenny held up his glass. "But them days you talkin' about is gone. Freeze is dead. Black and Bobby are businessmen. So whether you and me think that Nick was careless and should have taken Mylo's gun, that nigga runs this shit now."

"Well, maybe I ain't all that satisfied with Nick's leadership."

"And I guess you think you could do a better job?"

"I know I can."

Kenny took a sip of his drink and shook his head. "So why don't you kill Nick and step up," he said and laughed a little.

"Maybe I will. When the time is right," Bo said and put down his glass. He turned and looked at Kenny. "When that happens I need to know where you stand."

Kenny laughed. "I don't even know why I bother to fuck with you, Bo," he said and started to get up. "What you gonna do when Black comes after you?"

"If Black don't see that Nick had to go, then maybe Black gotta die too."

"You are crazy," Kenny said and got up from the bar.

On his way out of the club, Kenny ran into Cruz Villanueva. He was the nephew of Hector Villanueva, whom Black had dealt with many times. Black had known Hector since the old days when they both worked for André Harmon. Black did Hector a favor that cost Black money, but allowed Hector to buy cheaper and better quality product—a favor that put Hector in the position of power. His move to Miami only made that position stronger—a favor that Black called in when Shy needed to buy cheaper and better quality product from Hector.

"When I met you, we discussed a business arrangement," Shy said to Hector that day in Miami. "I wanted to know if the offer was still good."

Hector paused for a minute and looked at Shy. "You know I used to live and do business in New York. I still have many friends and many business associates there. Some have told me about the problems you are having. In fact, they tell me that just last night you took another loss. Is this true?"

"Yes. But I am moving to correct that situation," Shy said quickly.

"Shy, it hurts me deeply to tell you this, but I must retract my offer."

"Why?"

"You're not a good risk at this time. Please understand, once you have settled these matters I would have no problem extending the offer," Hector said.

"Just like that?"

"Well of course you can always do it all on the front end."

"I can't do that."

"Yes, I know, due to your problems. Of course, if Black were to guarantee your investment that would eliminate all of my objections."

"Hector, you better than most know. As a matter of principle, I will not do that," Black said. "And you insult me by mentioning it."

"My apologies, Black," Hector said bitterly. "Once again, Shy, I'm sorry we can not work together."

When Black saw the disappointed look on Shy's face, he knew that he had to do something. "Well, Hector, I do have a better idea." Shy and Hector both looked at Black.

"I'm listening," Hector said.

"It's simple," Black told Hector that day in Miami. "You extend to her the same deal that you offered her."

"No, Black!" Hector shouted. "Only if you stand with her."

"Hector, listen to me. All I am asking is that you stand behind your word. I know that you are an honorable man."

"Understand me, Black. I can't do that," Hector said as Shy looked on, feeling left out of her own business.

"Hector, look at me," Black said, looking Hector in the eyes. "I would consider it a personal favor if you would stand behind your word and do this for her."

Hector sat back in his chair and pondered Black's proposal. Shy sat quietly, looking back and forth at both of them. Finally, Hector said, "Shy, it would be my pleasure to do business with you." He got up from the table and handed Shy a card. "Call this number in New York when you are ready to do business. It is always a pleasure to see you, Shy. And you, Black, I hope this concludes our business together," he remarked as he and his associate walked away.

As they walked away Shy looked at Black curiously. "You mind if I ask you a question?"

"Sure, I knew you'd have questions," Black said, continuing to watch Hector until he was out of sight.

"Well, thank you. I only have a few questions. First of all, what just happened?"

"Hector owed me a favor."

"What was that?"

"I introduced him to Angee."

Black explained how back in the day, Hector used to buy from André, who was killing him on price. Hector knew he could get a better price from Black's friend Angelo Collette. One night while Black was at his club, The Late Night, Angelo came in. He talked with Black while Hector looked on and waited for his chance. When Angelo went to entertain himself with the ladies, Hector came running up to Black and begged him to introduce him to Angelo.

"Hector; let me make sure I understand you. You buy from André, who pays me. And now you want me to introduce you to Angelo, so you can stop buyin' from André, who pays me. Is that what you're asking me? Let me make sure I understand you. You want me to take money out of my pocket to help you. Is that what you're sayin', Hector?"

"Yes, Black," Hector said.

"You owe me a favor, Hector."

"Okay," Shy said.

"So I take Hector over to Angee and I say, 'Yo, Angee, this is Hector Villanueva. He's an honorable man and deserves to be taken seriously.' So Angee dismisses the honey he's talkin' to. He says to me, 'Is he a good guy, Mikey?'"

"I said, 'I wouldn't introduce him if he wasn't.' That's why he owed me."

"That's what all that honorable man stuff was about. You were reminding him that he owed you," Shy said.

"You catch on quick, college girl," Black said.

"Now, did you fuck his wife?" Shy asked, praying he'd say no.

"Yes," Black said to Shy.

Black had been having sex with Hector's wife, Nina, for a year, but didn't know she was married. She never wore a ring, and Black never asked her any questions.

"I never called her. I never even knew her number. She never knew mine. I'd see her around, we'd hook up, then I wouldn't see her for a while," Black said.

"So when did you find out she was married?"

"I saw her one night on the street, and she walked up on me. We talked for awhile then she says, 'Oh shit, here comes my husband.' So I'm like, 'You're married; to who?' And she points at Hector. I never saw her again after that day."

After Hector found out about the affair, he sent Nina to Miami so his family could watch and insure her fidelity.

When Hector moved to Miami, he very violently carved out a spot for himself. Cruz had worked for his uncle for years, but craved the power his uncle possessed. Hector knew that sooner or later Cruz's need for power would bring them to a point when Cruz would try to assassinate him. Together, they made the decision to send Cruz to New York to expand his business. When Cruz came to New York, he took over the drug trade in the South Bronx. Now he's set his sights on making a move uptown.

"You not leaving already, are you, Kenny?" Cruz said as Kenny passed.

"Yeah, I was about to get out of here," Kenny said and Luke and two of his men stepped closer.

"Stay and have a drink with me. I got something I want to talk to you about."

Kenny signaled for his men to back off. Luke put his gun away and took a step back. Kenny stepped to the bar. "What could you and I have to talk about?" he said and sat down at the bar.

Cruz signaled for the bartender. "Bacardi and coke, and bring my man whatever he wants."

"Chivas on the rocks."

The bartender left and Cruz leaned closer. "I been thinkin' about takin' my program uptown. I got the product and the people to make it happen. The only thing stopping me is Stark."

"Why tell me?"

"Everybody knows that Black stands behind Stark."

"I don't know what you're talkin' about," Kenny told Cruz, but he knew exactly what he was talking about.

As a favor to his long-time friend, Angelo Collette, Black agreed to take what Angelo referred to as, "A little more than just an introduction from you, Mikey."

"Like what?" Black asked Angelo that night.

"I was thinkin' that maybe you would take more of an active role. You could be kind of a stabilizing influence. You know, keep problems down. Naturally you can charge a fee for your service," Angelo suggested, and then he added, "I would consider it a personal favor."

Angelo considering his involvement a personal favor caused Black to reluctantly go against his convictions. "Angee, I can't get involved for my own reasons, but what I will do as a personal favor to you, is offer advice and counsel to Stark. And should the need ever arise; I'll act as an intermediary to resolve any disputes. You got a problem with him, you come to me. But understand, this is not a service. This I do for you out of friendship. I will not accept a fee. But for reasons that I know you understand, I can't go any further than that."

After that, the word got around that Black was the power behind Stark. Words that even though they weren't exactly true, Stark did nothing to dispute.

The bartender returned with drinks for Kenny and Cruz. When he left, Cruz continued, "Even if you say you don't know what I'm talkin' 'bout, everybody knows that Black is Stark's muscle, and that means you."

"What do you want, Cruz?" Kenny said, becoming more and more annoyed by the conversation.

Cruz turned away and took a sip of his rum. "I hear a lot of things."

"Like what?"

"Like maybe you ain't too happy with the way things are going and might be willin' to listen to another offer."

"So, I'm listening," Kenny said, even though he knew that no matter what Cruz had to offer, he wouldn't be interested. There was no question of his loyalty to Black, but Kenny thought he needed to know what Cruz was planning.

"You come work for me. I could pay you twice what Black does."

"That's not gonna happen; and if you try to move up-town, Black will crush you like the roach you are," Kenny said and turned to walk away.

"Don't walk away from me," Cruz said and grabbed Kenny by the arm.

Kenny pulled out his gun and shoved it in Cruz's face. "You ever touch me again, I'll kill you," he said, and Cruz let go of his arm.

"This ain't over," Cruz said as Kenny walked away.

"Yeah, and your mama ain't a two-dollar ho." Kenny gathered his men and they left the club.

"Yeah," Cruz said and drained his glass. "You one mutha fucka that's gonna have to be dealt with."

Outside the club, Kenny and Luke got in Luke's car. Luke's men got in another car and followed them from the club. They had driven a few blocks when another car cutoff the car with Luke's men, and ran them into the cars parked along the side of the street.

Luke looked in his rearview mirror at the accident and was about to turn around to see if either of his men were hurt. He saw two men get out and open fire on the car. "Did you see that shit," Luke yelled, when a Ford 350 pulled up behind his car. The big truck slammed into his rear end.

"What the fuck?" Luke said.

Kenny looked back. "Here they come again," he yelled as the 350 rammed them again. "Get us out of here," Kenny encouraged.

COMMIT TO VIOLENCE

Luke stepped on the gas and tried to get away from the truck, but the truck kept coming. The 350 slammed into their car again. The force of the impact forced Luke to hit his head on the steering wheel.

The truck stayed on the car's tail and ran it off the street into a telephone pole. Kenny and Luke jerked forward and were forced back by the impact of the airbags. Three men got out of the truck armed with AK-47s and opened fire. Luke got out of the car and was immediately hit in the shoulder. Luke dropped his gun. Then he caught another round in his thigh. Luke went down.

Still dazed from the collision, Kenny got out of the car. He got off a couple shots and then tried to get away from there, firing as he ran. The three men fired back and followed. When Kenny turned to fire again all three men let loose, and Kenny fell to the ground.

He was dead.

CHAPTER THREE

Rain Robinson walked through the crowd at JR's on the way to her office. She had taken over the club after her father, Jasper Robinson, died from complications of a stroke. JR was old school; a gambler that ran a few spots, including two major ones. The biggest was located in a warehouse that made machine parts, and another in the basement of the club. With her father dead and her having no interest at all in gambling, Rain turned over JR's gambling spots to Nick for ten percent off the top. She preferred to make her money in the dope game; which was something that her father disapproved of while he was alive, and she promised Nick she was done with.

For the most part, things were going well for Rain. At twenty-three, she was the queen in her world, and Nick was her king. She was introduced to Nick in that very office by her father. "Nick, this is my daughter Lorraine. Lorraine, this is Nick Simmons, he's an associate of Mike Black."

Rain sat behind what was now her desk and remembered how she smiled that night—like somebody told her that she had just hit the number. "I've heard a lot about you, Mr. Simmons. It's an honor to meet you."

"It's Nick, and it's good to meet you too, Lorraine."

She got wet from just the sound of his voice. "Call me Rain."

At the time, Nick was trying to rundown the bandits who robbed one of their legitimate businesses and killed two people. Nick heard that some of JR's people might have been involved. Rain saw it as her opportunity to get close to him and settle a few things of her own. "I can take you to the place where they hang out."

"I don't need you to take me anywhere," Nick told Rain that first night. "You just need to tell me who they are and where to find them."

"No deal."

"What you mean, 'no deal?' This ain't no fuckin' negotiation," Nick said. "You gonna tell me what I need to know and I'll take care of it."

"Good luck findin' them without me then," Rain said. She knew respect isn't given, respect had to be earned. And she had to earn Nick's. "Look, Nick, these is my people. I'm the one needs to make this right. Not you, me. So here's how it's gonna go. Me and you gonna roll by they spot, and I'm gonna handle my family's business."

It began there, but it didn't go down easy, at least not at first. "If the mutha fuckas that robbed my joint belong to you, and you wanna put your house in order, that's cool. You call me when you put a bullet in their brain."

"Look, nigga, I'ma say this one more time. Only mutha fuckin' thing I can tell you is that this nigga be hearin' shit. Now if that ain't good enough for you then pull

16

this bitch over and let me out. I'm tryin' to help your mutha fuckin' ass and you givin' me this shit 'bout it."

Rain had to laugh when she thought back on their first night together. She picked up the remote and turned on the big screen. A porno flick called *2 Ho's and a Bro* with Jada Fire, Havana Ginger, and Nat Turner exploded on the screen. She liked watching porn; it got her in the mood for Nick when he came by the club to check on the gambling operation.

She sat there waiting on Nick to come fuck her, watching the flick and thinking about the first time they had sex. How she felt her nipples brush against his chest. She knew that she wasn't the prettiest woman, but her body made men weak. Rain remembered Nick's eyes meeting hers then dropping to her titties. Rain touched his face and then she kissed him. When Nick stepped away from her he saw somebody at her window with a gun ready to shoot.

Nick grabbed Rain by the shoulders and pushed her down behind the couch. As the gunmen pumped bullets through her window, they stared into each other eyes. "I want to fuck you so bad," Rain said while the bullets flew over them.

When the shooting stopped Rain jumped up and ran toward the front door. She grabbed a gun from the lamp table by the door and ran out after her would-be assassins, firing wildly in their direction as the two men ran down the street.

It fascinated her sometimes how violence, especially gunplay, turned her on and made her want to fuck, but it did.

There was a knock at the door.

Rain had installed a series of security devices since she'd taken over. That included a camera outside her office. She picked up the remote and changed the display on the big screen.

There stood Blue Claxton, who ran the gambling in the basement of the club. He was one of the few people that Nick allowed to stay after he took over. Rain assured Nick that Blue was a very loyal soldier to JR, and she thought that he could be trusted to represent her interest in the operation. Rain pressed a button to allow him to come in the office. "What up, Blue?"

"Ain't nothing," Blue said and went straight to the bar.

"Pour me one too."

"Patrón?"

"For sure."

Blue poured the drinks and handed the Patrón to Rain. "I hear Jay Easy got out," he said and sat down in one of the chairs in front of her desk.

"I heard that too. So, how's it goin' tonight?" she asked and took a sip.

"Mutha fucka hit us for ten grand tonight at the crap table and bounced. Come to find out he was playin' with loaded dice," Blue informed her and shot his drink.

Rain seemed unconcerned. "Nick will be here in a minute. Make sure you tell him."

"Tell Nick?"

"What; you ain't hear me? Tell Nick."

"You don't give a fuck about this shit, do you?"

"We got cameras everywhere so I know we got video on this mutha fucka. If he's out there to be got, Nick's people will get him."

"Nick's people? Damn it, Rain, this is your shit! Your daddy and Jeff Ritchie worked hard buildin' this business; too hard for you to just give it away to that nigga."

Rain opened her desk drawer and was about to pick up her gun. Then she looked at Blue and closed the drawer. "I ain't gonna get into this shit with you, Blue. I got too much other shit on my mind to have you fuckin' wit' me."

"So I heard."

Rain lit a cigarette and blew the smoke in Blue's face. "What you heard?"

"I know all about your little dope business. You know your daddy didn't like that kind of business."

"My father is dead."

"And I know he must be rollin' over in his grave 'bout the shit you doin'."

"What you know about what I'm doing?"

"You mean other than givin' away your father's business? I know that you took that money and used Nick's connections to get yourself in business with Bruce Stark."

With two of his former partners, Kevin "K Murder" Murdock and Steven "Cash Money" Blake, dead, and Billy "BB" Banner in the wind, Stark was in a rebuilding phase. Rain saw that as an opportunity. She went to Stark with a proposal.

"Look, nigga. I know you tryin' to recover from your little Commission fallin' apart."

"What business is that of yours?" he asked her.

"I could help you with that. I got the money and the people in place to step into that void."

"You?"

19

"Yeah, me, mutha fucka. What, you don't think I can handle mine?"

"It ain't that I don't think you can handle your business. I heard some things about you, so I know you can. But you're with Nick now."

"What that got to do with this?"

"I know you two are partners in your father's gambling joints."

"And?"

"And I gave my word to Black that I wouldn't involve him in any of my thing."

"Come on now, Stark, don't bullshit me. I know Black got his hand in your business."

"You don't know shit," Stark told her.

Rain didn't like the way he said it. It was like he didn't respect her or her position.

"Black don't have shit to do with my business and I'm not gonna sit here and explain it to you. If you was all that you play it like you are to Nick, you'd know what the deal is between me and Black."

Rain took a deep breath and picked up the gym bag she had with her. She sat it on the table and opened it. "You mean to tell me that you gonna let this money walk out of here tonight?"

Stark leaned forward and looked in the bag. He got up and went to the bar he had setup in the corner of the room. "You want a drink?"

"Patrón if you got it," Rain answered.

While Stark poured he thought about the bag of money sitting on his coffee table. He knew Rain was right; in the position he was in, he couldn't let that much money walk. He handed Rain her drink and sat down. "What you gonna do when Nick finds out about what you're doin'?"

"Who gonna tell him? You? I know I ain't gonna tell him a mutha fuckin' thing."

"You know word gets around on the street. Sooner or later the nigga is gonna hear that Double R is back. And she out there with product."

Rain sat back in her chair and took a sip of her drink. Stark was right about that, niggas will talk. She thought for a minute. "Niggas won't know it's me behind this shit. All they'll hear 'bout is some nigga named PR."

"PR?"

"That's right, nigga, PR. They'll think it's some Puerto Rican mutha fucka or some shit like that. They won't even know if it's a man or a woman."

"This can't come back on me in any way, Rain."

"Trust me, nigga, it won't," Rain assured him.

"It better not, because if you fuck up my business with Black, I'll—"

Rain leaned forward. "What you gonna do, nigga?"

Stark leaned forward and zipped up the bag. He got up and took the bag with him. Rain sat quietly and watched as Stark handed the bag to one of his men.

"See Moon on your way out, he'll take care of you. From here on, you deal with him. You and I don't talk anymore. And one more thing—"

"What's that?" Rain frowned.

"You have no credit here. No money, no product," Stark said and went in another room and closed the door behind him.

21

Rain stood up. "Nice doin' business with you." *Bitch nigga,* she said to herself and went on with Moon that night.

For a while things went smoothly. Money was flowing and she was able to keep any knowledge of her involvement in the game from Nick.

That ended the week before when somebody robbed two of her spots. She had lost five of her people. Murdered; execution style. They were killed on their knees with their hands tied behind their backs. Then the killers shot them twice in the head. Rain knew that she would have to deal with that, but not that night.

That night she had smoked a blunt, had a couple of shots of Patrón and was waiting on Nick to come knock her back out. She wasn't in the mood for any shit from Blue.

"Why don't you worry about runnin' these spots and makin' this money and let me do what I do. Unless you tired of makin' this money," Rain said.

"You don't get it, do you, Rain?" Blue said and dropped his head. "You never did." Blue finished his drink and stood up. "It ain't always about the money."

"You sound like a fuckin' fool. What's it about, if it ain't about the money?"

"It's about honor and loyalty to the people you got history with. Not that mutha fucka Black. We don't need them niggas. We did just fine without them all these years."

"Don't make me regret keepin' you around, Blue," Rain said and put her hand on her gun again.

"Keep me around?" He started walking toward the door. "Maybe when you get a little older you'll realize that you can't just use people and throw them away when you're done with them."

"Whatever, nigga," Rain said. She was startled by a loud banging on her office door. She looked at the big screen and saw Mixson, one of her dealers, leaning against the door.

Rain pressed the button and Mixson fell in the office. Rain jumped up and Blue rushed to him. Blue pulled him in the office while Rain closed the door. Blue helped Mixson into a chair. Rain looked down and saw the trail of blood; then she noticed the cuts on his face and knew that she'd gotten hit again.

"What happened?" she asked.

"There were four of them; caught us by surprise."

"How'd you get away?" Rain wanted to know, since nobody had survived the other two robberies.

"I just started bustin' shots and when the shit got too thick, I jumped out the window."

"So you don't know what happened, do you?" Rain asked and picked up the phone. When she got no answer she dialed another number and got the same result. She turned back to Mixson. "I guess they're all dead."

Blue looked at Rain. "So is he."

CHAPTER FOUR

Bobby Ray held up Rawls' head and hit him again. He was tied to a chair and for the last hour, Bobby had been hitting him in his face, his chest, and his arms. No matter how much or how hard Bobby hit Rawls, he hadn't said a word.

Mike Black sat quietly and watched Bobby work. Every once and awhile he would get up and ask Rawls the question. "Where is Ebony Washington, and where are the papers she was carrying?" When Rawls didn't answer, Black would walk away and Bobby would go back to work.

Black sat down and took a deep breath. He thought about the reason he even knew or cared who Ebony Washington was. It was just after eleven o'clock when Black got a call from Martin Marshall. Martin was a United States Congressman who Black was in business with.

"Black, it's Martin. I need your help."

"What is it now, Martin?" Black asked.

"One of my people was kidnapped earlier tonight, while she was carrying some very important papers."

"What does this have to do with me, Martin?"

There was silence on the phone before Martin finally said, "The truth is I got careless, Black."

"Get to the point, Martin."

"You remember our meeting with Chang and the Cubans?"

"What about it?" Black said and thought back to that meeting and how it led to him getting shot. He remembered Martin coming to him with a plan to invest in sugar-based ethanol in Cuba.

They met a few days later in the Bahamas with Silvestre de la Toribio representing the Cuban Foreign Trade Ministry, Soberón Nicodemo Plácido representing the Cuban Sugar Industry, and Maximino Cristóbal. He was representing a group with oil interests in Venezuela.

At that meeting the debate raged on about whether to invest in sugar-based ethanol or in oil production between Cristóbal and Plácido, until Chang had heard enough. "Would you gentlemen excuse us for a moment or two?"

Once Cristóbal, Plácido, and Toribio left the room, Chang turned to Martin. "What do you think my friend?"

"For my money, ethanol production is the only way to go. I didn't come here to talk about oil."

"I must say that I agree. What do you say, Jiang?"

"Ethanol is the future, and we must look to the future."

"What about you, Mr. Black?" Martin asked and all eyes turned to him.

"Like the man said, when the oil is gone, it's gone. You can always grow more sugar cane."

"Then we are in agreement," Chang said and stood up. He went to the door and asked the others to come in. Once they had reclaimed their seats, Chang told them of their decision. "At this time, gentlemen, we feel that it is in our long-term interest to make our investment in ethanol production."

Plácido and Toribio shook hands and seemed to be very happy with the decision. But Cristóbal, on the other hand, was not. He rose to his feet. "I think you gentlemen are making a big mistake." The next time Black saw Cristóbal was the day he got shot.

"You remember that I was taking notes," Martin said. "Well, when I got back, Ebony, my assistant, the one they kidnapped, she got my notes and created a memo of that meeting and filed the memo in a folder called Cuban meeting."

"Damn, Martin, how could you let some shit like that happen?"

"I'm sorry, but now you see why you have to help me get those papers back. Your name is all over that memo. You know what will happen if it becomes public that a United States Congressmen and a gangster were meeting with officials of the Cuban government in violation of American-Foreign policy? You said it yourself, it's illegal. Treason-type of illegal."

"You know who got her?" Black asked.

"I don't know who they are, but I have an idea where they might be. When they called about the ransom, they stayed on the line too long, and I was able to trace the call." Martin gave Black the address where the call was made.

"Okay, Martin, I'll get your memo back," Black said.

"And the woman too," Martin insisted.

"What's more important; the memo that'll send us to prison for treason, or the woman?"

"Both. Ebony is very important to me. I love her, Black."

"Wait a minute, Martin. These guys kidnapped your mistress? Do they even know what she was carrying and what it means to you?"

"It's possible, but I doubt it," Martin said. "That means you need to get to them before they read it."

When they arrived at the address Martin gave them, Black and Bobby went to the door and Rawls was coming out. He was carrying a woman's coat and one shoe. Both matched the description that Martin had given Black of what Ebony was wearing when they had dinner earlier that evening. They forced Rawls inside at gunpoint, tied him to a chair and searched the house. Ebony wasn't there. That was over an hour ago, and they were no closer to finding her.

Bobby hit Rawls in the face and took a step back. He looked down at Rawls' feet. "Those some nice kicks there. What kind are they?" Bobby asked.

"Stacy Adams," Rawls mumbled.

"Can I see them?" Bobby asked and knelt down to take the shoes off. He walked over to where Black was sitting. "These some bad-ass kicks, Mike. I gotta get me a pair of these." He turned back to Rawls. "What size are these?" But Rawls was too out of it to answer.

"I don't think he's paying you any attention, Bob," Black said and laughed.

"Hey asshole," Bobby yelled and threw a shoe at him. "I'm talkin' to you." The shoe hit Rawls in the face, but he still didn't answer.

"Told you." Black laughed. "He doesn't respect you, Bob. He thinks that you'll get tired of hitting him and you'll go away, and he won't have to tell you shit."

Bobby walked up to Rawls, picked up the shoe and hit him in the face with it.

"What are you—his mother now? Beatin' him with a shoe," Black laughed, but Bobby didn't seem amused. He was getting frustrated with Rawls. Bobby was doing some of his best work, and he hadn't said a word.

"You think you a tough son of a bitch, don't you?" But Rawls still didn't answer. "Well, dickhead, we'll see just how tough you are in a minute," Bobby said and walked away. "You wait right there."

"Where you goin'?" Black asked.

"Garage."

There was silence in the room for a minute or two before Black got up and dragged the chair he was sitting in closer to Rawls.

Rawls raised his head and looked at Black. He knew Black was right about him. Rawls was counting on Bobby getting tired. Rawls figured that after a while Black, who appeared not to think that he was going to talk, would pull Bobby off and go try to find Ebony without his help. But Rawls had no idea who he was dealing with, or what they were capable of doing to get what they wanted.

"You know it's only gonna get worse from here, right?" Black said. "I mean, he's gonna come back from that garage with some bazaar shit to beat your ass with. You know that, right? Now I've known Bobby for a long time, and I know he's not gonna stop until you tell us what we wanna know. Save yourself a lot of pain and tell me where Ebony Washington is, and where are the papers she was carrying. 'Cause once he gets started, I may not be able to stop him."

Bobby came back in the room carrying a sledge-hammer and an ax. "Too late for that shit now, Mike. He done fucked around and made a nigga mad."

"I tried to warn you," Black said and moved out of Bobby's way.

"I don't give a fuck if you don't say another word. You gonna die slow, bloody and painful tonight." Bobby dropped the ax and swung the sledgehammer over his head and brought it down on Rawls' kneecap.

Rawls screamed and Bobby hit him in the other knee-cap.

"That sounds like it hurts," Black said. "I think you better tell this nigga something."

"Fuck that, Mike. He ain't got to say shit to me for the rest of the night," Bobby said as he hit Rawls in the chin. "I'm about to go Kunta Kinte on his ass." Bobby dropped the sledgehammer, knelt down in front of Rawls and pulled off his sock. Then he shoved the sock in Rawls' mouth. "The time for talkin' is over." Bobby got in Rawls' face. "It's party time."

"Look at him, Bobby. He's all confused and bothered. I don't think he knows what you're gonna do. I mean, I don't think he saw *Roots*."

Bobby picked up the ax. "Well, he's about to find out." He knelt down in front of Rawls again and grabbed Rawls' ankle. "This is gonna hurt."

"No shit," Black said as Bobby brought the ax down and chopped off Rawls' toes.

As Rawls grimaced in pain and the blood oozed out of what was left of his foot, Bobby went in the kitchen and came back with a knife. Then he ripped the sleeves off of Rawls' shirt and made long incisions down his arms. "Now we gonna see if you bleed to death before I cut your throat."

Mike walked back over to Rawls. "You sure you don't want to tell me where Ebony Washington is and where the papers she was carrying are?" he asked, but didn't bother to take the sock out of his mouth.

"Mike!"

"What?"

"If you not gonna help, get the fuck out my way."

Black shrugged his shoulders and took two steps back. Bobby stepped in front of Rawls and began punching him in the face with hard lefts and rights. Once his hands started hurting, Bobby picked up the sledgehammer and began ramming it into Rawls' chest. Rawls could hear his ribs cracking. Slowly he began to realize that he was going to die, just the way Bobby said he would, slow, bloody and painful.

"Damn, Bob. I heard that shit. I think you broke his ribs," Black said.

"You wanna hear bones breakin'? Watch this," Bobby said and came down with the hammer on Rawls' arm with so much force that it broke the arm of the chair. Rawls opened his eyes and looked at the blood and his bone sticking out of his arm. He bit down harder on the sock because the pain had become more than he could stand.

Bobby walked around to the other side of the chair and was about to do the same to the other arm when

Rawls pushed the sock out of his mouth with his tongue. "Okay—okay, shit! I'll tell you what you wanna know."

"Fuck that!"

Bobby raised the hammer over his head, but Black grabbed his arm. "Let's hear what the man has to say, Bob."

"Okay," Bobby said, but as soon as Black let go, Bobby brought the hammer down on Rawls' other arm. While he screamed in agony, Black looked at Bobby and shook his head. "No point wasting a good swing."

Once again, Black pulled his chair closer to Rawls. "Where is she?"

"Brooklyn—in a house on Sterling Street. They got her in the basement."

"How many men are with her?" Black asked.

"Three: two upstairs, one in the basement watching her."

"What's the plan?"

"I'm supposed to meet them there later with the money, and then we'll let her go."

"Good man. Now where are the papers she was carrying?"

"I don't know," Rawls said. He really didn't know. He had no idea what papers Black was asking him about all night. All he knew was that when they brought her in, she wasn't carrying anything.

"I'm getting tired of this," Black said and stood up. He kicked Rawls in the chest and the chair fell over. Black went in the kitchen and got the biggest pot he could find. He went to the sink and filled the pot with water.

Black came back to the living room to find Bobby standing over Rawls kicking him in the face. "Bobby!"

"What?"

"I'm in the middle of something here," Black said and stood over Rawls with the pot of water in his hands.

"Sorry."

When Bobby stepped aside, Black started to pour the water slowly in Rawls' face. Rawls turned his head to one side, trying to keep the water from going in his mouth and up his nose.

"Hold his head, Bobby."

"But I'll get wet," Bobby laughed.

"Bobby!"

"All right, all right, you don't have to yell," Bobby said and kicked Rawls again. Then he got down and grabbed his face with both hands. Black tilted the pot slowly and water began to rush down on Rawls' face. With Bobby holding his head, he couldn't avoid the rushing water. When the pot was empty, Bobby stood up and kicked Rawls again.

Black dropped the pot and knelt down next to Rawls. "Where are those papers?"

"In the garage." Rawls thought if she had the papers when his men took her that, that was the only other place that he could think the papers might be. At this point, Rawls was ready to tell them anything they wanted just to get them to stop. "Trunk of my car," he said, still gasping for air and spitting water out of his mouth.

"Thank you," Black said and stood up. "Let's go," he said to Bobby and they headed for the garage.

"Hey! Wait a minute. You can't leave me like this," Rawls yelled until he heard the door close.

"Water boarding?" Bobby asked. "That was your big move?"

"Hey, if fuckin' Dick Cheney can do it, so can I. Besides, it worked, didn't it?"

Black went around to the back of the car and shot out the lock in the trunk. He picked up the briefcase and opened it. Black quickly flipped through the papers until he found the one he was looking for. He started to leave. "Wait a minute, Mike."

"What?"

"You just gonna leave him in there?"

"Yeah. He'll bleed to death, and that'll be that."

"Yeah, but suppose somebody comes lookin' for him?"

"You're right," Black said, took out his gun and went back in the house. He walked over to Rawls and stood over him.

"Thank you," Rawls mumbled.

Black raised his gun and shot Rawls twice in the head. "You're welcome."

When they arrived in the house where Ebony Washington was being held, Bobby parked the car in front of the house and turned to Black. "So what's your plan?"

"I been thinkin' about that. Thinkin' what would Monika do?"

"Shit, sexy one-eye would blow the place up and tell Martin that we couldn't save his ho."

"I thought about that too. I mean, we got the important shit and that was the memo."

"Right."

"But I promised Martin that I'd bring her back alive. He's in love with her," Black said and got out of the car.

"Since I ain't plannin' on dyin' for love, what you gonna do? You just gonna open the gate, walk up the steps, ring the bell and ask them to send her out?"

"Something like that. Come on," Black said and opened the gate. On the way up the steps, both Black and Bobby took out their guns and put their silencers on. Black rang the bell and they stepped to either side of the door.

"Who is it?" a voice came back.

"It's Rawls. Open up."

As soon as the man opened the door, Black shot him in the head. They entered in time to see a man come out of the living room. He fired two shots at Black and Bobby then ran up the stairs.

"I got him," Black said. "You go find Ebony."

Black followed the man up the steps just as he ran into a room. When Black entered the room, the man came out from behind the door and knocked the gun out of Black's hand.

Black turned around and kicked the gun out of the man's hand before he got a shot off, and punched him in the face. Then he grabbed him by his belt and his collar, and threw him through the glass and out the window.

When Black got back downstairs, he saw Bobby coming out of the basement with Ebony. "What happened?"

"When I got down there, one of them was holding her with a gun to her head," Bobby said as they walked out the door.

"What'd you do?"

"I shot him," Bobby said.

"Who are you guys?" Ebony asked.

"It's all right, honey. We're friends of Martin Marshall. He sent us to find you," Bobby said as they passed the man Black threw out the window. His body was draped over a metal fence with a spike coming out of his back. "What happened to him?"

"What does it look like? I threw him out the window."

"Just askin'."

CHAPTER FIVE

Mike Black sat in his office at Cuisine and waited for Bobby and Nick to get there. When he got the call from Cynt that Kenny and three of his men had been murdered in the street, he was shocked, then he got mad, and then he became reflective. Black thought about those he'd lost over the years; and two inparticular.

Losing his wife Cassandra was probably the hardest thing he ever had to deal with in his life. There were times when no matter what he did or how hard he tried, he could not stop thinking about her. Although the time he recently spent in the Bahamas with CeCe allowed him to have some closure about her death, Cassandra and the great love he felt for her was still never far from his thoughts.

But as hard as that was to deal with, at times like this, it was Freeze that he missed. As much as he hated to admit it, he had made a mistake putting Nick in charge. It wasn't that things had gone all that wrong. It was more that Nick didn't have the same feel for the job that Freeze brought to the work.

Nick never wanted the job, Black pushed it on him. For his part, Nick would have been perfectly content to takeover the high-stakes poker game that Jackie Washington now ran for him. Maybe that's what he should have done, and made Jackie continue to work with Travis and Monika on the very-lucrative projects they brought to the table.

Recently, changes in the global economy forced Black to rethink their push to go completely legitimate. They had lost a lot of money on some of the investments that they made with Meka Brazil. Meka's understanding of the business climate in this country led her to believe that the best opportunity for long-term investment existed offshore. "China, India and even Russia are where the growth markets are at this point," Meka told them at their last meeting.

Black liked Meka; thought she was smart. He hadn't even mentioned his new Chinese-backed investment group to Meka, and she was already looking in that direction. Black didn't blame her for the major losses they took. There was no way she could have anticipated the changes in the market. At least she hadn't invested in credit default swaps or mortgage backed securities, which played a factor in bringing the markets down.

For the time being, Black had decided that he would have to put plans for business expansion to the side. Now was the time to focus his attention on the real money maker. From his point of view, the recession had improved rather than hurt his business. *Hard times make people more likely to gamble and men more likely to buy more pussy tryin' to escape from reality,* he thought as Bobby and Nick came in.

"I guess you've heard?" Black asked.

"Any idea who did it?" Bobby asked.

"No," Black said. "I just heard about it."

"I got everybody out askin' questions," Nick said. "But so far, nobody's heard anything."

"Somebody knows something," Black said. "You need to find them and make them tell you what you want to know."

"I'm on it, Black." Nick assured Black.

"Ain't that Detective Harmon over there in the corner?" Bobby noticed.

"Looks like him," Black said. "What's he doin' here?" he asked.

"He's here to see me," Nick said. "The detective is doing some work for me."

"What kind of work?" Black asked.

Nick looked at Black. "You wanna hear about this?" He asked Black, knowing that he was trying to stay out of the day-to-day stuff.

"I do," Bobby said definitely.

Black nodded his head. He would tell both Nick and Bobby of his decision to step back in, later.

"Bo's got something goin'—something big. And he forgot to tell me about it," Nick continued.

"What's the deal?" Bobby asked.

"I don't know. That's what I got Harmon lookin' in to."

"You sure you can trust Harmon?" Bobby asked.

"I've done business with him before," Nick told them. "Let's see what he's got. I'll be right back.

Until a month ago, Jack Harmon was a decorated New York City homicide detective. He was under investigation for use of excessive force. The charges were dropped, but not before Jack ran up a huge legal bill. It was only by chance that he ran into Nick and told him about a surveillance job. "It pays five grand," Nick told Jack that day. Being broke, Jack couldn't say no.

"What you got for me, Jack?" Nick asked as soon as he sat down with the detective.

"Your boy Bo is doing business with the Russian mob," Jack said.

Nick sat back in his chair. Bo having a deal with the Russian mob was the last thing he expected to hear. "Ex-KGB agents, veterans of the Afghan and Chechen wars; out-of-work but with skills that are useful to criminal organizations," Nick said and thought about how useful his military experience had been to him.

"Bo's contact is a guy named Nikolai Mikhailov. He's a member of the Izmaylovskaya Gang.

"Never heard of them," Nick said and signaled for a waitress.

"They're considered one of the country's most important and oldest Russian Mafia groups in Moscow," Jack said. "But they operate here in New York, in Tel Aviv, Paris, Toronto, and Miami."

"How strong are they?"

"My information says they're estimated to consist of about anywhere from three to five hundred active member's worldwide. It's run on a quasi-military style and strict internal discipline."

"What are they into?" Nick asked.

"They're involved extensively in murder-for-hire, extortion, and infiltration of legitimate businesses. A lot like you guys."

"When is the job goin' down?"

"Tonight at ten."

Nick looked at Jack, took an envelope out of his pocket and put it on the table in front of him. Jack opened the envelope and peeked inside. "Thanks, Nick. This will help out a lot with my legal bills. Any time you need info like that, you give me a call," Jack said and got up.

"Anything else I can do for you, Jack, you let me know," Nick said and rejoined Black and Bobby. He wasted no time telling them who Bo was doing business with.

"Bo had made a deal to deliver high-end vehicles to the Russian mob," Nick said. "Ever heard of the Izmaylovskaya Gang?"

"I think I might know somebody connected to them," Black said.

"You mean that Russian you and Angelo drink with sometimes?" Bobby asked.

"That's right. He's ex-KGB turned showdown artist."

"He fits the profile," Nick said.

"This really doesn't create a problem for us, does it?" Bobby asked.

"Not from where I'm sittin'. Doin' business with the Russians is a good thing," Nick said. "Only problem is Bo thinkin' he could get something like this done and think nobody would know about it."

"How'd you find out about it?" Bobby asked.

"Victor's fuckin' Sabrina," Nick said and laughed.

"That pillow talk will fuck up a nigga's program every time," Bobby commented. And he was absolutely right.

"The only time she can get away from Bo is when he got something goin'. She tells Victor, he tells me."

40

"What you gonna do about Bo?" Black asked. He knew the minute he told Bo that Nick was in charge that this was coming.

"Don't worry, Black, I can handle Bo. He can't make a stray nickel with me knowing about it."

"That ain't what I mean. There are some people whose respect you'll never earn, Nick. You can't have a mutha fucka like that in your house. Sooner or later you'll have to deal with him before he comes after you."

"Mike's right, Nick," Bobby added. "Just him tryin' some shit like this, it gives other niggas the idea that they can do it too."

Black thought about Freeze. "You know what Freeze would do?"

Nick laughed. "He would go over there right now and kill Bo."

"I ain't sayin' that's what you should do. You handle Bo any way you want. All I'm sayin' is sooner or later you're gonna have to deal with him."

"I understand," Nick said and got up. "I'm gonna go have a talk with Bo."

"You do that. And then I want you to see what you can find out about Kenny."

"I'm on it," Nick said, and Black watched him as he left Cuisine.

"Who do you think's gonna move first?" Bobby asked.

"My money's on Bo."

"Word I get is that Bo thinks he should be running things, and he blames Nick for Freeze bein' dead," Bobby said.

"I heard that too. That's why I told Nick he's gonna have to kill Bo. But he needs to decide that for himself."

"You're right," Bobby said and sipped his drink. "Where you goin'?" Bobby asked as Black got up.

"Goin' to see if I can find out anything about what happened to Kenny."

"Didn't you just send Nick to do that?" Bobby said and followed Black toward the door.

"So I wanna ask a few questions myself," Black said. "What else you got to do?"

CHAPTER SIX

When Black and Bobby got outside, they got in Bobby's car. They had driven for a while and Black noticed that Bobby was uncharacteristically quiet. Since he had a lot on his mind, Black didn't mind, but there was a question he had to know the answer to.

"What's bothering you?"

"Nothing," Bobby replied as he drove.

"Nothing, huh? Well, let me ask you this then; what was up with you last night?"

"What you mean?"

"I mean you chopped the guy's toes off with an ax."

Bobby laughed. "The shit worked, didn't it?"

"That's not the point."

"Well, what's the point then?" Bobby asked angrily.

"I just never saw you like that before, that's all," Black said and decided it was best to back off.

They had driven for a while in silence when Bobby looked at Black and said, "Pam wants a divorce."

"That's what's bothering you."

"And she's talking about moving to South Carolina with the kids."

"That's fucked up. What did you do this time?"

"I got home one night and the house was fucked up. I mean, shit was thrown everywhere. I looked around for the kids, but they were gone. I finally found Pam sitting in the basement. She said some woman called the house asking for me."

"Same old Bobby. Didn't you learn shit from fuckin' around with Cat?" Black asked referring to the last woman Bobby had an affair with.

Cat decided it was a good idea to call Pam and tell her that she had just gotten finished fucking Bobby, and he would still be there if Black hadn't called and asked Bobby to pick him up. That forced Pam to have to deal with the situation in a way that nobody ever thought she was capable of.

After that, Pam had a nervous breakdown. When she got out of the hospital, she told Bobby that even after what he put her through, she could be a good mother to the children and a good wife to Bobby, but she couldn't bring herself to have sex with him.

After that, they came to an understanding. Pam understood that if she wasn't gonna give Bobby any pussy, somebody else would. "Just keep it away from me and the kids. I won't go through what I went through again," Pam told Bobby. And that was fine with him. So it was settled. Bobby did his thing and kept it away from his family. Until now.

"Yeah, I did, but I swear, Mike, it ain't like that this time."

"What's her name?"

"Ivillisa Ortiz. Little Puerto Rican ho I fucked a couple of times. I don't even know how she got my number."

"What she say to Pam?"

"Nothing; just asked to speak to me, and if she saw me to tell me that she'll be at home waitin' for me."

"That's a little more than nothing, Bob. It was enough to set Pam off and make her tear up the house and ask for a divorce."

"No shit."

"What you gonna do now?" Black asked as Bobby pulled the car over.

"I don't know," Bobby said and put the car in park.

"Your choices are simple. Either you're gonna be what Pam wants or you're not."

"No shit," Bobby said and started to get out of the car. "You coming?" he asked and got out of the car.

They went inside the convenience store and walked up to the young woman at the counter. "He here?" Black asked.

"He's in the back," she said and pointed.

"Thanks," Black said and headed for the back.

"Hey, Bobby," the woman said flirtatiously.

"Hey, Debra," Bobby winked and followed Black.

"What? You fuck her too?"

"Prettiest titties I ever saw, but she couldn't fuck her way out of a paper bag," Bobby said.

Black shook his head and opened the office door. Bobby followed him in.

"Black; Bobby," Sherman Williams said and stood up to shake hands. He had been running numbers out of that store for years. Sherman also had a reputation for keeping his mouth shut and his ears opened.

"What's goin' on, Sherman?" Bobby asked.

"Money. Lots of fun and lots of money. Same as every other day. What brings you two high-rollers up here?"

"You heard about Kenny?" Black asked.

"Yeah, I heard about it. Shame, too—dirty shame. Kenny was good people. Honest as far as that goes in this business."

"You heard anything about who killed him?" Bobby asked him.

"I ain't heard shit about Kenny. But I tell you what I have been hearin'. And I can't say that it had anything to do with Kenny, but I keep hearin' it from a lot of people—people who know what's up—that something big is gettin' ready to go down around here," Sherman told Black and Bobby.

"That does us a lot of fuckin' good," Black said. "Something's gonna happen, something big, but you don't know what."

"Sorry, Black, that's all I got, but I'll let you know if I hear anything else."

"You do that."

"Have you talked to Luke?"

"No."

"I did hear that he was with Kenny last night when it happened."

"Why didn't you tell us that shit before?"

"Sorry," Sherman said as he watched Black and Bobby walk out.

CHAPTER SEVEN

When Nick got to JR's, Rain was more than ready for him. She was all over him as soon as he walked in her office. Once she had gotten her fill, Rain got dressed and ready to go. "You don't mind if I ride, do you?"

"No, come on," Nick said and turned around. Rain followed him out of the club and to his car; neither had much to say to the other while they drove. Rain sat and stared out the window, thinking about what Blue had said to her. *I know he must be rollin' over in his grave 'bout the shit you doin'.*

When Rain was young, JR took her everywhere with him. That's why she was so much like him. Back then she was daddy's little girl and there was nothing more important to Rain than pleasing her father. But as she got older things began to change. Rain was always in trouble and her brother Miles, the straight-A student, became JR's favorite. No matter what Rain did to impress him it was always wrong. "No, Lorraine, do it this way," she remembered JR telling her so many times in her life.

She knew her father wouldn't approve of what she was doing. It was always like that. If it wasn't exactly what JR wanted it was wrong. But JR was dead and Rain had to do what she knew how to do; what she'd always done. Having money and power behind her just made things easier, and her association with Nick gave her that power. It was the perfect arrangement except for one thing.

Wanda Moore.

Whenever Rain would get a little too comfortable with Nick, Wanda would always come along to jerk her back to reality. It didn't bother her when they first got together. But every time Nick would get out of her bed to go be with another woman, it would remind her that Nick was Wanda's man and she was just the bitch he was fuckin' behind her back.

"What we doin' here?" Rain asked when Nick pulled up in front of Clay's Garage.

"Something's goin' on and there are people that don't think I know what's goin' on."

"Bo."

"We're here to show them that I know everything," Nick said and got out of the car. Rain put one in the chamber and followed Nick in the building.

Clay's Garage was a car cloning operation that's been run for the last couple of years by Bo Freeman. From Clay's Garage, Bo runs the operation where a stolen cars' vehicle identification numbers, or VIN, were replaced with ones that belong to legally obtained vehicles. Bo's men washed car titles clean by using the internet to get vehicle identification numbers from similar makes and models that had been salvaged, then put new VIN plates on the stolen cars' dashboards and created matching titles. They then re-registered the cars in

North Carolina, South Carolina and Georgia, where bar codes on New York titles can't be read.

They were also stealing an average of 25 cars a week and selling the parts through salvage yards in the tri-state area. The dismantling and stolen parts operation was run by Hank Jackson. He would receive orders for specific vehicle parts and give orders to various "steal men" to steal the appropriate vehicle in order to obtain the requested parts. Once the vehicles were stolen, they were taken to Clay's where they were dismantled. The requested parts were then taken to the various auto body shops that had ordered them.

For Bo and Hank, tonight was a big night. Bo had made a deal to deliver a predetermined list of high-end vehicles to members of the Russian mob. The cars were taken from a storage facility where a number of car dealerships stored their excess inventory and then drove the vehicles to various lay-up locations. If everything worked out, tonight would be a big night.

Bo looked at the clock on the wall in his office and then at Sabrina. "What time is it?" she asked.

"Eight forty-five. Why, where you gotta be?" Bo asked.

"Nowhere," Sabrina lied. There definitely was somewhere she had to be, and a certain time that she had to be there. "Nowhere but the bed."

That part was true.

She had a little more than an hour to get where she was going. At ten-thirty she wanted to be between the sheets with Victor Lewis between her thighs. Sabrina knew if Bo didn't leave there soon that she would be late.

COMMIT TO VIOLENCE

At thirty-seven years old Sabrina Cole was a very beautiful woman. Even when the occasional black eye she'd received from Bo forced her into big sunglasses. She had been with Bo for twelve years since she arrived in New York from Mississippi. In that time she had two years of good and ten years of bad. Sabrina had been sneaking around with Victor for the last six months and for the first time in ten years, she was happy. Sabrina had her a young thug and he was putting it on her.

Victor was twenty-four and made his money running numbers and collecting for Nick. He had been in love with Sabrina since the first time he saw her. To Victor, Sabrina was the most beautiful woman he had ever seen. Whenever he would have a chance to be anywhere she was, Victor would watch her from a distance. He loved the way she talked; slow, sexy and just country enough to turn him the fuck on. It took him two years to get up nerve to talk to her when Bo wasn't looking. Come to find out while Victor was watching Sabrina, Sabrina was watching him.

For the next six months they sniffed around one another; flirted and teased one another until one night Victor caught Sabrina alone at a club. She had just had an argument with Bo because she had the nerve to comment on the fact that she caught him openly flirting with another woman while she was sitting right there, and she thought that was disrespectful. After that Bo left the club. Then she saw Hank walk up to the woman Bo was flirting with. They talked for a few seconds before she got up and followed Hank out of the club. What pissed Sabrina off was that she smiled and waved at her before she left to be with Bo.

Never far away and always on the lookout for any opportunity to be with Sabrina, Victor came and sat down next to her.

Sabrina was so caught up in her anger that she didn't notice Victor until he leaned in close and said, "Hello."

Sabrina was startled when she heard his voice, but the sound of it made her happy. "Hello, Victor."

"Bo shouldn't leave you alone like this."

"I think Bo has other things on his mind right now."

"His mistake. That would never happen between you and me."

"And why is that?" Sabrina asked and leaned close to Victor.

"Because you are always on my mind."

"You know, Victor, you always say the nicest things to me," Sabrina said and smiled.

"You know I'd do anything to see that smile."

"Why don't you take me home? See how nice you can be to me," Sabrina told Victor that night. It's been on since then. Any time that Bo had a job to do, Sabrina would make arrangements to meet Victor.

Sabrina looked at Bo. She knew that he would be busy for hours. She allowed her mind to think about Victor taking his time and making love to every inch of her body. All that needed to happen now was for Hank to say they were ready to go.

"What's wrong with you?" Bo asked.

"Nothing. I'm just tired, that all."

"Why don't you go on home then?"

"That's all right," Sabrina said. "I'll stay with you until it's time for you to go."

"For what? To sit here and do nothing? Go on and get outta here. I'll get with you tomorrow."

Sabrina smiled to herself when she heard that. She stood up and tried her best to look mad. "So I'm not gonna see you later?"

"Gonna be hung up with things most of the night. I told you that."

"All right then, call me tomorrow," Sabrina said and picked up her coat. She gave Bo a goodnight kiss on the cheek and left the office.

Just as she was about to open the door to leave, Nick walked in with Rain.

"How you doin', Sabrina?" Nick asked.

"I'm fine, Nick," Sabrina said and give him a hug. Then she hugged Rain. "I like that outfit, Rain."

Sabrina never liked Wanda since day she called her a country bitch. So the idea that Nick was fucking Rain behind Wanda's back gave Sabrina some satisfaction.

"Thank you," Rain said to Sabrina. "You lookin' good, as always."

"Bo here?" Nick asked.

"He's in the office," Sabrina said and pointed to the office on her way out the door.

When Hank saw Nick he headed for the office to tell Bo. "We got company, Bo."

Bo looked up and saw Nick and Rain walking around watching his men load cars onto cargo carries. "What he doin' here?" Bo said and got up.

"I don't know. You think he heard about what we got goin' tonight."

"Why else would he be here," Bo said and followed Hank out of the office.

"How you think he found out?" Hank asked.

"How you think?" Bo asked and turned to face Nick. "What's up, Nick?"

"Bo; Hank," Nick said and looked around the garage. "You hear about Kenny?"

"No, what happened to Kenny?" Hank asked.

"Somebody killed him last night."

"Damn," Bo said and paused. "I saw Kenny last night at The Beat."

"What time was this?"

"Around eleven, eleven thirty," Bo said and looked at Hank for confirmation. Hank nodded.

"You see who he was with?" Nick asked.

"He was with Luke and that other nigga, I forget his name," Bo explained. "We had a few drinks then he left. But on the way out he stopped and talked to Cruz."

"Cruz?"

"Cruz Villanova," Hank said. "You know, Hector's nephew from Miami. Whatever they talked about, it ended with Kenny shovin' his pistol in that mutha fucka's face."

"What happened after that?" Nick asked.

"Kenny left," Bo said.

"What about Cruz, he leave after that?"

"Can't really say. It wasn't too long after Kenny left that we left and came back here. You think Cruz killed him?" Bo asked.

"I don't know. I would like to know what they were talkin' about. Ask around. See what you can find out."

"You got it."

"By the way, lotta cars in here," Nick said and took a step closer to Bo.

53

"Yeah," Bo said.

"Lot more than usual."

"Yeah."

"So I guess I'll see Hank tomorrow sometime?"

"Yeah, Nick, you'll get yours," Bo said and took a step back.

"Good."

Nick turned and started walking away. Rain stepped up to Bo. "Good to see you niggas," she said and walked away laughing.

"Yeah, mutha fucka. You gonna get yours. Count on that," Bo said.

"How he find out about this shit?" Hank asked.

Bo turned and looked at Hank. "How you think he found out. One of these niggas talkin'." Bo looked around the garage at his men. "Don't matter," he said as he watched Nick and Rain leave the building.

"What you wanna do?" Hank asked.

"Get the rest of the cars loaded up and let's get outta here."

"I mean about Nick?"

"I'm gonna have to kill him," Bo said and went back in his office.

Having accomplished his purpose, Nick walked back to his car. Once he and Rain had driven a little ways, Rain asked a question. "How'd you know Bo had something big goin' tonight?"

"You don't know?"

"No. How you know?"

"I know everything," Nick said and smiled at her.

No you don't, nigga. Your ass don't know every fuckin' thing, Rain thought and smiled back. There was a lot going on in Rain's life that Nick didn't know about. Most of it, Rain knew she needed to tell him about. She looked at Nick and knew that this was not the time to tell him about her problems.

"What's up with you and Bo anyway?" Rain asked.

"What do you mean?"

"I mean it's obvious that you don't like him, and that mutha fucka hates you."

"Two things."

"What's that?"

"He blames me for Freeze," Nick said.

The truth was Nick wasn't mad that they blamed him for Freeze's death, because he blamed himself. They were both caught off guard when Mylo went for his gun. "How come he still had his gun," was the question Bo shouted at Nick at Freeze's funeral, and Bobby had to separate them.

Nick asked himself over and over, why didn't they take the gun from Mylo when they caught up to him? There was only one answer to that question: They both got careless; a mistake that cost Freeze his life.

Why did I let him get away? Why didn't I shoot Mylo? Why didn't I go after him? All Nick could think of at that moment was that he couldn't leave Freeze. He had to get help for him. "Somebody call an ambulance!" But it was too late. Freeze was dead before they got to the hospital.

No matter how many people told him so many times that it wasn't his fault, Nick felt responsible. It was a burden he would carry for the rest of his life.

"You said two things, what's the second?"

"Bo, and some other people, thinks he should have got this spot after Freeze died. Not the man that got him killed."

"What you think about that?" Rain asked, and Nick didn't say anything. "Okay. Why did Black choose you over Bo?"

"Trust. Black couldn't do what he's doin' now and not be able to trust him completely."

"What that mutha fucka think was gonna happen? You and Black got years together."

"Yeah. But it's more than just years," Nick said. "I told you, it's about loyalty and trust."

Rain thought about loyalty and trust and her situation with Blue. She had known Blue for as long as she could remember. Over the years, he had been a loyal soldier to her father's right-hand man, Jeff Ritchie. But did that mean he was loyal to her? And if Blue wasn't loyal to her, could she really trust him?

"Did Blue talk to you?" Rain asked as they drove.

"No more than he usually does. Why?"

"He's about to get on my last nerve."

"What he do this time?" Nick asked.

"He came to me yesterday and said that some mutha fucka was playin' wit' loaded dice and hit us up for ten G's."

"And they let him walk outta there?"

Rain didn't answer.

"I been tellin' you for the longest that Blue runs a sloppy operation. Shit like this keep happening maybe you'll believe me."

"Believe me; I'm startin' to agree with you. Maybe it is time for him to go."

"You're the one that insisted that we keep him."

"I told you, Blue was a real loyal soldier for my father. I thought he'd be the right one to watch out for my interests."

"I'm lookin' out for your interests,"

"You are, aren't you," Rain said and thought about her real problem. After getting hit twice, she was running low on product and money. Rain had to do something and she knew she needed help. Telling Nick was the last thing she wanted to do. Not that she didn't think he would help her. Rain knew she could get Nick to do anything she wanted. She just didn't feel like hearing his mouth.

CHAPTER EIGHT

Bobby turned on White Plains Road and headed back uptown. Each place they stopped, nobody knew anything about Kenny's murder. After talking with Sherman, Black and Bobby went by Luke's apartment, but he wasn't there. Black told Bobby to ride by there again to see if he had come back.

"So what you think about this big thing Sherman was talkin' about?" Bobby asked as he drove.

"I don't know, Bobby. I'm just hopin' whatever it is doesn't involve us."

"Yeah, me, too, but I got a feelin' that it does."

"You know I hate it when that happens 'cause you're usually right. You think somebody's comin' after us?"

"Killin' Kenny may have been the first move."

"Happens every time," Black said.

"What's that?"

"Every time we step back a little, somebody sees that as weak, and they try us."

"Then we kill them; and everything goes back to normal. It's the natural order of things," Bobby said.

"Yeah, I guess so," Black said and looked out the window.

The fact that he couldn't keep living this way was never far from his mind. Black thought about how he was shot and almost died at a meeting with legitimate businessmen.

It began when Congressman Martin Marshall called and said he wanted to meet to talk about a new business opportunity. Black and Martin usually met on the corner of 34th Street and 7th Avenue. They blended into the crowd and talked. "I'm thinking about making a little investment, and I need a partner."

"I'm listening."

"How much do you know about sugar-based ethanol?" Martin asked.

"Not much."

"I'm thinking about making an investment in Cuba."

"Isn't that illegal? Like treason-type of illegal?"

"That's why I need partners. You being one, and some Chinese businessmen," Martin announced.

"That supposed to make me feel better about it?"

"With its huge potential for producing clean, renewable sugar-based ethanol, Cuba represents a significant source of energy that will remain unavailable to American consumers unless we undo the embargo."

"Is our new president moving in that direction?" Black asked.

"He's already relaxed some restrictions," Martin told Black that day. Martin went on to explain how the huge potential for profit would be if the Cuban ethanol would become available for export to its nearest neighbor.

"I see your point. What's the next step?" Black asked.

"I'm going to arrange a meeting with my Chinese friends and some enterprising members of the Cuban government."

"When?" Black asked.

"I'll call you in a couple of days, and I'll let you know where and when."

"I'm going to the Bahamas day after tomorrow," Black said. He had made arrangements to meet Jamaica in Nassau to talk about expanding and to look into buying some property on the island.

"Bahamas, huh? Business or pleasure?"

"Little of both."

"How long are you planning on being gone?"

"Couple of days. I'll keep in touch."

"Do that," Martin said and the two separated.

One advantage to meeting Martin on 34th Street was that it served a dual purpose. It was far from Martin's Congressional District in the Bronx, and it was close to a high-end boutique called The In-town Experience, which was owned and operated by CeCe. Her real name was Cameisha Collins. She used to be with a baller that called himself Cash Money. After Cash was murdered by Mylo's hit team, CeCe made herself very useful to Black. Anything he'd tell her to do got done.

Since he was going to the Bahamas, Black decided to invite CeCe to join him. "That is if you're not too busy," he said, looking around the practically empty store.

"Just you and me?"

"You, me, and Kevon."

"Of course I want to go with you. How long are we staying?"

"Couple of days. Maybe a week.

After spending a few days in Nassau, Black met Martin in Freeport for their meeting with the Chinese and the Cubans.

"Martin Marshall to see Huang Chang." Scotty, Martin's right-hand man said. And the man stepped aside to allow them to enter. When they entered the suite, two men and a very attractive woman all rose to their feet.

"Mr. Marshall," one of the men said and extended his hand. "I am Huang Chang. This is my associate, Wei Jiang. My assistant Mei Ai Bao and you have already met Xiang Yong. He is, how you say—my bodyguard," Chang said and each bowed slightly.

"This is my associate Mike Black. You've already met Scotty, and this is Mr. Black's bodyguard, Kevon Bailey."

The meeting was a success. The group decided to move forward and make an investment in Cuba, while Martin used his position to influence American foreign policy. But there was one person at the meeting who was not happy with the decision. His name was Maximino Cristóbal. He felt strongly that the group should invest in oil development in Cuba instead of sugar-based ethanol.

Chang had just returned from his trip to Cuba and was anxious to get together with Black to discuss the details of their venture.

"To be honest with you, Chang, I was making plans to get off the island before you called," Black told Chang. There was a hurricane reported to be heading for the island, and he wanted to be gone before it hit. "Why don't we get together when we get back to New York? This way Martin will be able to sit in with us."

"Here is the situation. I spoke with Cristóbal several times while I was in Cuba. He is still here on the island. He still feels that we should make an investment in oil development."

"I understand that. It puts him in a better position financially. But we all agreed. Oil is not where the future is."

"And that is still my position. That has not changed. As you said, when the oil is gone it's gone. You can always grow more sugar cane."

"Exactly," Black said. "So if that's the case, why are we even talking about oil?"

"I only agreed to speak with him as a courtesy to Clemente Eustaquio. As I said, Clemente is a trusted old friend, whom I have done business with for years."

"I can understand that."

"I assure you that we will take care of our business and be off the island long before the storm approaches."

"So when does he want to get together?"

"This afternoon over lunch, so please bring your associate with you. Martin tells me that she is quite charming, in addition to being very beautiful."

Black looked at CeCe who was sitting across from him packing. "She is that *and* so much more."

"After that, I am leaving the island going back to New York on my private jet. I would be honored if you would join me."

"I accept your most gracious offer."

"Excellent. My limousine will pick you up at your hotel at noon."

"We'll be ready."

The meeting was to be held at a house in McLean's Town, which was about forty kilometers outside of Freeport. It was the farthest settlement on the east end of the island that could be reached by two roughly paved roads. The winds were stronger on that side of the island as the storm approached much faster than anyone had anticipated.

When they got to the house, lunch was served and afterwards, Black, Chang and Cristóbal went into another room to talk. Kevon, CeCe and Chang's assistant, Mei Ai Bao were asked to wait along with two of Cristóbal's men. Xiang Yong, Chang's bodyguard waited outside along with another one of Cristóbal's men.

"Cuba has been oil hunting for decades, and their attempts have not always been successful," Chang began as they entered the room.

"This is true," Cristóbal said and took a seat behind his desk in front of the French doors. "However, as you know, with discovery of oil field's revealed within five miles of Cuba's northern coast, we expect yields which could excess forty percent of Cuba's total production," Cristóbal said.

"How much is that?" Black asked.

"Roughly seventy-five thousand barrels a day of heavy crude. Oil companies from China have already begun talks with Cuban energy officials about investments in deep-water operations."

"I am well aware of this fact, Cristóbal," Chang said and looked impatiently at his watch.

"What you may not be aware of is that the north Cuban basin holds a substantial quantity of oil: ten billion barrels of crude and ten trillion to twenty trillion cubic feet of natural gas. This creates an opportunity for foreign oil conglomerates with offers of production-sharing agreements."

Chang took a deep breath. "You tell me things that I am already well aware of. And frankly, it does nothing to change my mind in this matter."

"I am sorry that you feel this way," Cristóbal said and pushed a button on his desk.

"I agreed to meet with you today out of respect for Clemente. But unless you have something new and profitable to share with us, I'm afraid this meeting will be a short one," Chang said.

Outside the house one of Cristóbal's men approached Xiang Yong and motioned him for a cigarette. When Xiang Yong stood up, the man covered Xiang Yong's mouth and shoved a knife in his stomach.

Back inside of the house. "Clemente was an old fool who had outlived his usefulness." Cristóbal removed a gun from the desk drawer and stood up. "That is why I killed him," he said and shot Chang.

Cristóbal turned the gun on Black and he hit the floor quickly and took out his gun. Hearing the shot, Kevon burst through the door and was immediately shot twice in the chest. Black fired at Cristóbal, but he was able to escape through the French doors.

In the living room, one of Cristóbal's men shot Mei Ai Bao and started toward the office while the other went after CeCe, who had just come out of the bathroom when the shooting began. She quickly went into one of the other rooms and hid under the bed.

Black got to his feet and went after Cristóbal. When he got to the doors, Black could see him running and fired at him, but missed. Black came back inside and saw one of Cristóbal's men standing over Kevon's body. He looked at Black and both men fired. Black hit him with two shots to the head, but felt pain and burning in his stomach.

He kicked the gun away from Cristóbal's man and knelt down next to Kevon. He checked for a pulse. "Goodbye, my friend," Black said and closed his eyes.

Black picked up Kevon's gun and went into the living room. He saw Mei Ai Bao's lifeless body slumped over on the couch, but no CeCe.

"CeCe," he screamed and went looking for her.

Black opened the front door and saw Xiang Yong's body. "Damn." He looked around to see if he saw her and went back inside. Knowing that there were at least two more of Cristóbal's men as well as Cristóbal himself, Black moved through the house slowly.

Cristóbal's men separated and began going room to room looking for CeCe. One had just checked a room and came back into the hall when he spotted Black. But Black saw him first and let loose with both guns. The man went down. Black took his gun and shot him twice in the head before moving on.

"CeCe," he called again, but got no answer. Though he tried not to think about it, his mind drifted to thoughts of Cassandra. He couldn't let another woman die because he wasn't there to protect her. He gripped his guns a little tighter and continued his search, hoping that he wouldn't find her dead.

Cristóbal's man finally made it to the room where CeCe was hiding under the bed. She held her breath and tried to remain as still as possible. She had heard

Black calling for her, so she knew he was coming. She just hoped that he would get there before it was too late.

CeCe watched the man's feet as he moved through the room looking for her. She closed her eyes when he stopped in front of the bed. "There you are, bitch."

CeCe opened her eyes and saw the gun pointed at her. She shut her eyes tightly, and then she heard the shot, then another, and then a loud noise. She opened her eyes and saw the man lying on the floor next to the bed.

Black turned the bed over and held his hand out to help CeCe get up. "Are you all right?" Black asked.

CeCe got up and threw her arms around him. "I'm okay."

"Come on. We gotta get out of here," Black said and dropped to his knees.

CeCe looked at him and saw the blood on his shirt. "Oh my God! You've been shot!"

CeCe struggled, but was able help Black to his feet. She draped his arm over her shoulder and helped him walk out of the room.

"Where's Kevon?"

"He's dead," Black said as he walked. He could feel himself starting to get light-headed, most likely from the loss of blood pressure. By the time they got to the door, he felt like his legs were about to give out on him.

CeCe could feel the weight of his body increase on her shoulders. "Hold on, baby. I'm gonna get you outta here."

As they got closer to the door, they could hear what sounded like more shots being fired. They stopped.

Black took a deep breath and raised his weapon. "Get behind me," he said.

"It sounded like it was coming from outside," CeCe said, and they continued making their way through the house. When they reached the door Black leaned against the wall and looked out the window. "Do you see anybody?" CeCe asked.

"No. But it's hard to tell with all that rain. Wait here." Black opened the door and stepped outside with his gun raised. CeCe followed him out, having to step over Xiang Yong's body.

"We got to make it to that limo," Black said. He started to walk, but his legs were giving out and he had to steady himself against the wall to keep from falling.

"No," CeCe said and took Kevon's gun from his waist. "You stay here and save your strength. I'll get the car."

"You know how to use that?"

"No, but it will come to me," she said and ran out into the pouring rain toward the limo.

Black kept his gun raised and watched as CeCe made it to the limo. She stopped in front of the limo and looked back at him. Then she moved around to the side, and then around to the other side. CeCe opened the driver's side door and stepped back quickly. When Black saw her running back toward the house, he knew that something was wrong.

"The driver is dead. All four tires are flat, and there's a big hole in the front."

"Cristóbal. That was what that shooting was," Black said and CeCe helped him back inside.

"What now?" CeCe said.

"Get the phone from Kevon's pocket. Jamaica's number is programmed. Call him and tell him to come get us."

"That could take a while, especially in this weather," CeCe said.

"You got a better idea now's the time," Black said to CeCe and they waited for Jamaica to come with a doctor to save his life.

Maybe Bobby was right, this was just the natural order of things. It was the same in both of his worlds. People will do anything to get what they want, even if they have to kill to accomplish their goals.

CHAPTER NINE

Black looked out the window as Bobby drove to Luke's house, and his mind drifted to Kevon. He thought about Jiang, one of the Chinese businessmen. After he was shot in Freeport, they talked at Kevon's funeral. "How are you feeling my friend?" Jiang asked.

"Much better."

"That is good to hear."

"I am sorry about Chang, Mei Ai Bao and Xiang Yong," Black said.

"They will be missed. Chang was like a brother to me. I will feel his loss for many years."

"I hate to ask at a time like this, but how is Chang's death going to affect our business with the Cubans?"

"I'm sorry to say that without Chang, there is no business with the Cubans. The contacts were his; contacts he spent years developing. With Chang dead, the Cubans will most assuredly turn to Cristóbal to do business."

"Cristóbal knew that, and that's why he killed Chang."

"I agree."

"Where is Cristóbal now?"

"I know what you are thinking, my friend, but Cristóbal also killed Clemente Eustaquio."

"I know. He told Chang that before he shot him."

"He has consolidated power in a town called El Peronil and has a small army protecting him, which makes him almost impossible to get to."

"Nobody is impossible to get to."

"This is true. However, now is not the time. Now is the time for patience. But I assure you, this act of dishonor will not go unpunished. In time, we will have our revenge," Jiang shook Black's hand and walked away.

"Fuck Bruce Lee," Bobby said. "When we going down there?"

"Jiang is right. If he is protected like that, gettin' his ass is gonna take time and planning. And I know the perfect person to set it in motion." Black looked at Bobby and smiled as Monika walked up.

For the next two weeks, Black remained in the Freeport, recovering from his wounds and enjoying being with Michelle and CeCe. When he felt that he was well enough to travel, Black and CeCe went to his new house in Nassau. But after a few days they both agreed that they missed being with Michelle. The next morning Black got up and left early and came back that night with Michelle. Over the next three months, Black enjoyed his life with his girls until a visitor arrived.

"Hello, Monika," CeCe said when she answered the door. She led Monika through the house and out to the pool. When they got outside, Black was with playing in the pool with Michelle.

While Monika took a seat at poolside and set up her laptop, CeCe got in the water to play with Michelle and Black got out to talk to Monika.

"Y'all just one happy family here," Monika mused.

Black looked at her then continued to dry himself. "What you got for me?"

"For last three months, I've had an operative in El Peronil keeping an eye on your boy Cristóbal. He lives on a three acre compound," Monika said and pointed to the satellite image on the screen. "It's surrounded by an electrified fence, and he's protected by a militia of at least thirty men."

"Okay, how do we get to him?" Black asked.

Monika zoomed in on the image. "On the back side of the compound there is a heavily wooded area. That's how we'll make our approach. The trees will give us enough cover to get to the main house without being detected."

"How close?"

"We'll clear the trees about two hundred yards from the house." Monika sat back in her chair. "Now, once we clear the trees there is a foot patrol we need to neutralize and two guard towers. Once that's done we'll approach the house, go in, and get Cristóbal."

"How many men in the house?" Black asked.

"No way to be sure how many will be in the house at any given time."

"Sounds pretty formative, but you wouldn't be here unless you had a plan, so let's hear it."

"My team will fly into Santiago Pérez Airport in Arauca, Colombia. From there we will make our way by car to the border, enter Venezuela and head for El Peronil."

Monika took out a map. "This road will take us close to the property here," she said and pointed. "Then we'll continue on foot for ten clicks to the penetration point at the fence. We'll make camp there, because I plan on taking them at four-thirty A.M."

"What about the fence?"

"My operative will deactivate that section of the fence so it looks to anybody that's monitoring like it's still active. We'll cut the fence and go in. Like I said, once we clear the trees, we'll neutralize the foot patrol and two guard towers, go in, and get your boy."

"What about the militia? How are you gonna handle them?"

"They're housed in this building here. At the time we plan on hittin' them, they should be asleep. I want to be in and out without them knowing. But I got a plan for them if it becomes necessary."

"I know you're not planning on hiking ten miles in the dark when you're done, so how we getting outta there?"

"Of course I have an exit strategy. We got a thirty-minute window to complete the operation. At five o'clock my operative will pick us up at the main gate and take us to an airfield where he'll have a plane ready."

"Who's your team?"

"Me, Nick and Travis."

Black shook his head. "I'm going with you. And so is Bobby."

"For some reason, I knew you were gonna say that." Monika laughed. "You sure you two, Bobby especially, are up to it?"

"He'll complain the whole way, but he'll be all right."

72

"But it's a ten-kilometer hike through heavy brush in one hundred degree heat."

"We're going. Make it happen," Black said and got back in the pool with his girls.

"Yes, sir," Monika saluted and packed up her laptop.

Two weeks later the team arrived at Santiago Pérez Airport in Arauca, Colombia and was met by one of Wei Jiang's men. He provided them with a van and weapons. From that point, they headed for the border.

When they got to the woods at the rear of the compound, they broke out weapons and machetes and proceeded to the objective. Along the way, as expected, Bobby complained the whole way. If it wasn't, "It's hotter than a mutha fucka out here." It was, "Are we there yet?" until Monika had enough.

She turned around and held up her machete. "Bobby, if you say one more fuckin' thing, I swear to God I'll cut your fuckin' head off."

"Lighten up, Monika. Take some deep breaths," Bobby said and kept walking. As the sun began to set, they made it to the fence.

"Okay," Monika said. "We camp here until it's time to make our move."

"I'm gonna checkout the area and set up a defensive perimeter," Nick said and walked off.

"The rest of you get some rest. We go at O-four-thirty," Monika said.

Bobby looked at Black and then to Monika. "Yes, sir," he said and saluted.

"Fuck you, Bobby."

"Anytime you're ready."

At O-four-thirty the team put on night-vision goggles, put silencers on their weapons and approached the fence.

"How do we know if your man did his job?" Bobby asked.

Nick picked up a small piece of wood and threw it at the fence. When nothing happened, Travis cut the fence and they went through.

Once they reached the clearing they got ready to make their move. "Nick," Monika said and got out her binoculars.

Nick broke out a Barrett 82A1 50BMG Semi-auto Rifle and took aim at the guard tower. With one shot, he took out the guard manning the tower. "Good shot," Monika said.

"Thanks," he said and took aim at the other tower.

Now that the towers were neutralized, they separated into two teams.

"Nick, you and Travis head for the barracks and rendezvous with us at the main house," Monika ordered. "Black, Bobby, you're with me."

Nick looked at his watch. "Give us five minutes before you move," he said, and Travis followed Nick to the barracks.

When they reached the barracks, Travis stood guard while Nick planted C-4 charges and remote detonators around the building. Then Travis saw the motor pool. "How much more C-4 you got?"

"Enough. Why?"

Travis pointed. "Motor pool."

"Good looking out. Come on," Nick said. Once the charges were set, Nick and Travis made their way to the rendezvous point.

Meanwhile, Monika, Black and Bobby approached the main house and were surprised that they didn't encounter any foot patrols. Shortly thereafter, they were joined by Nick and Travis, and the team entered the house. After walking through the first floor, they met at the staircase. Black and Monika were about to check the second level.

"Nick, watch the back. Bobby, you take the front of the house. Travis, you stay here," Monika said.

As Bobby made his way toward the front of the house, he heard a noise. "Somebody's coming in," he said. Monika moved quickly to the door while the others took cover. Bobby positioned himself on the other side of the door and waited.

One woman came in the house. Bobby grabbed her and covered her mouth. Monika shoved a gun in her face. "¿Yo no le doleré, comprenderá?" Monika said quietly in Spanish, letting the woman know that she wasn't going to hurt her.

"Si," the frightened woman said quickly.

"¿Dónde está Cristóbal?"

"Arriba," the woman said and pointed upstairs.

"Muéstrenos," Monika ordered the woman to show them and pushed her toward the steps.

The woman led Monika and Black up the stairs to a bedroom at the end of the hall. The woman pointed to a door. "Adentro."

Monika opened the door and then followed Black inside with their guns pointed. At the same time, Nick saw two men approaching the back door. He took aim with the rifle and fired two shots. Two bodies dropped.

Cristóbal was asleep, alone in the bed. They approached the bed quietly and took up positions on either side of the bed. When Cristóbal didn't move, Monika poked him with the barrel of her gun.

Cristóbal began to stir. "Good morning," Monika said and eased the gun to his head.

Cristóbal opened his eyes and saw the two of them. He recognized Black. "What are you doing here?"

"I came to kill you," Black said and shot Cristóbal in the eye. "Rest in peace, Kevon." Then Black put two shots in his chest.

Black looked at Monika. "This was too easy," she said as she left the room.

"We're not out yet," Black said and followed her down the steps.

"Everything all clear out front, Bobby?" Monika asked as Nick and Travis joined them at the door.

"All clear, general" Bobby said and saluted.

Monika gave him the finger. "Let's move."

While Monika led her team out single file towards the gate, they were unaware that a militiaman on foot patrol had discovered the bodies Nick dropped, and sounded the alarm.

When the alarm was sounded, lights came on in the compound. Militiamen that were stationed at the main gate began firing at them.

"So much for easy," Black said and fired. Bobby set himself and opened fire on the men at the gate, while Black and Travis took cover.

"Blow it," Monika yelled as she ran for cover with the rest of her team behind some cars that were parked in front of the house, and returned fire.

Nick detonated the charges he set at the barracks, but not before several men made it out of the building. They headed for the main gate.

When he heard the alarm followed by the explosions, Monika's operative started up his Chevy Avalanche and sped toward the gate.

Travis saw the men coming from the barracks as they made their way across the compound. He fired on them as they passed the motor pool.

Black and Bobby continued shooting as Travis set off the C-4 charges they had set at the motor pool. The explosion took most of them out. The ones who survived the blast took cover.

Monika's operative crashed through the gate. As the truck barreled toward them, Nick rose up and laid down enough cover fire for them to get in the truck, before he jumped in the flatbed and continued firing until they made it out of the compound.

As Bobby drove back to Luke's house, he looked over at Black. "What you thinkin' 'bout?" he asked.

"Venezuela," Black said and looked out the window. "Venezuela and the natural order of things."

"What about it?"

"Is that all there is?"

"All what is?"

"The natural order of things; is that all there is? People try to kill us, we kill them. I mean, is that all there is to life?"

COMMIT TO VIOLENCE

"As long as we're livin' this life, yeah Mike, that's all there is. Like I said, it's the natural order of things."

ROY GLENN

CHAPTER TEN

Rain banged on the steering wheel and leaned on the horn. She had been stuck on the Cross Bronx Expressway for almost an hour and she had barely moved a half a mile. She had made up her mind a half hour ago that she was going to get off at the next exit. At this point she could see it, but getting to it was still a ways off. When she finally was able to get off the expressway, Rain made her way to her destination on the surface streets.

She parked her car down the street from the building and walked down the street. As she got closer, Rain saw four men come running out of the building. They got in a late model, dark colored Chevy Blazer that was double-parked, and sped away. At the time Rain didn't think much about it; to her they were just in a hurry. She was right about that, but it was the reason *why* they were in such a hurry that would matter to her.

When Rain got to the apartment the door was cracked opened. Knowing that the door should be closed at all times, Rain took out her gun. She pushed the door open slowly, but really wasn't prepared for what she saw when she stepped inside.

There was so much blood.

"Damn," Rain said aloud. There on the floor lay three of her men. All with their hands tied behind their backs. Each shot twice in the back of the head.

Even though she knew the effort would be futile, Rain checked to see if the product was gone. She went in the kitchen and opened the freezer. It was empty, just as she thought it would be.

Rain got out of there and went back to her car. As she drove away from the building, Rain took a moment to think about the fact that if she wasn't stuck in traffic, she would have been there when the shooters got there. Part of her thought that had she been there things would have gone a different way. But the farther she drove, the more Rain realized that had she been there, she'd be dead now.

"Fuck!" Rain yelled and dug around in her purse and pulled out her cell. She dialed Nick's number.

"What's up, Rain," Nick said when he answered.

"I need to talk to you," Rain told him.

"I'm listening."

"Not on the phone. Where you at?"

"At Jackie's."

"Wait for me. I'm on my way."

When she got to the house where Jackie ran a high-stakes poker game, Rain told Nick what she had been doing.

"Damn it, Rain," Nick said and buried his head in his hands. "How long has this been goin' on?"

"Long enough," Rain told Nick and he gave her a look of disbelief.

How could he been so blind not to know what she had been doing? "Do you realize the position that puts me in?" he said without looking at her.

"This was my thing; I didn't involve you in it at all. Nobody even knows it was me behind them. Shit, even you didn't know. It ain't got nothin' to do with you."

"It has everything to do with me!" Nick shouted. "With all of this!"

"I'm sorry!" Rain shouted back.

"Sorry don't matter," Nick said. "Who's your supplier?" he wanted to know.

"Why you gotta know all that," Rain said defensively. The last thing she wanted to tell him was that she was buying from Stark.

"It don't matter." He got up and grabbed Rain by the shoulders. "It ends now. Right fuckin' now, you hear me?"

"I hear you, nigga, shit. But I need your help."

"Help with what?"

"Last couple of weeks four of my spots been hit. They took all the product."

"That's fucked up, but that's one more reason why it ends now. So I don't see what you need my help with."

"'Cause they killed my people. Tied them up and shot 'em in the head."

"That shit sound more like something personal if they killed your people."

"What makes you say that?"

"'Cause it takes time to tie mutha fuckas up and shoot them. Robbers wanna get what they came for and get outta there. Believe me, killin' mutha fuckas, that's the kind of shit you do when you wanna send somebody a message."

"How you know?"

Nick sat down on the couch in Jackie's office. "Me and Freeze were stickup kids. We'd hit two or three a night some times. And the money was good; three, four, five grand a pop for a minutes work. Most times we never had to fire a shot."

"I never knew that, and I thought I had heard every story there was about you and Freeze from back in the day," Rain said.

"Nobody knew it was us," Nick said and thought about it. He had heard about somebody named PR coming up in the game, but since it didn't concern him he didn't think much of it. Now he looked at Rain. "Just like nobody knows it's you, PR."

"What you say?" Rain asked.

"PR, that's you ain't it. Purple Rain," Nick said and shook his head.

"What you know about that?"

"I told you, I know everything," Nick told her. "Maybe you ain't as smart as you think you are, Purple Rain."

"Maybe I ain't. That's why I need you to help me get outta this."

"Yeah," Nick said.

There was one other thing. Rain's reluctance to tell him who she was buying from led him to believe that it was Stark. If that was the case, Stark would have to be dealt with. But for now, that would have to wait. As much as he hated to admit it, Rain was right. He had to help her and do it before Black found out what he was doing.

82

CHAPTER ELEVEN

It was late and detectives Kirkland and Richards had gotten a call about a triple murder. They had worked together on drug-related homicides for the last five years and Kirk was just starting to get comfortable enough with him to let him drive. Taking the lead in their investigations was another matter.

When they got the call, Richards was on the phone with his wife. She called to complain about their young sons. Complaining about how much of a handful they were becoming, and with him working so many crazy hours, it felt like she was raising them alone. He was glad to rush her off the phone.

"So what was it this time, Pat?" Kirk asked.

"Matt took apart the toaster."

Kirk laughed. "Why'd he do that?"

"Same reason he takes apart everything, to see how it works," Richards said as he drove.

"Makes sense."

"Yeah; right up to the part where it comes to putting stuff back together. The parts never seem to all get back in there and they never work right after that. Drives Helen crazy."

Kirk laughed but didn't comment. He'd learned years ago to stay out of his partner's marriages. Especially since his track record with wives wasn't stellar.

"How come you never had kids?" Richards asked.

"I've been married three times, but I never stay with one long enough to have any."

"Three wives. I gotta say, if this one doesn't work out, I'm not doing it again."

"I seem to remember sayin' that too. One thing I learned, you're married to the badge and after a while, your wife becomes a mistress you sneak and see when the badge allows it. I even tried marrying another cop this last time."

"How'd that work?"

"Lasted eight months. It was worse 'cause she was married to the badge too. Shit, we rarely saw each other and when we did, it was just to have sex."

"Sounds like the perfect marriage to me," Richards laughed.

"Not really, you still have the arguments. Now that we're divorced, we still have the same sex and we don't have to argue," Kirk said as they arrived at the scene of the murder.

When they walked in the apartment they were met by Detective Gene Sanchez from the narcotics division. "There they are," Sanchez said and walked them into the room where the bodies were found.

"What you got for us tonight?" Richards asked.

"Three black males murdered execution style. The lab guys saved the bodies for you."

Kirk crouched down next to one of the bodies. His hands were tied behind his back. Richards looked over the other bodies; each had been shot point blank in the back of the head.

"From the looks of it, they were on their knees when they were shot," Sanchez informed them.

"What do you think, Pat?" Kirk asked.

Richards nodded his head. "No sign of forced entry, so the shooters were let in. Judging by the bullet holes in this wall, somebody shot at them. Shooter fired back with superior firepower, I might add."

"You got anything on those guys?" Kirk asked and pointed to where the bodies were found.

"They weren't on our radar," Sanchez said.

"Anybody canvas the building?" Kirk asked.

"Uniforms."

"And?"

"Nobody saw anything, nobody heard anything. Nobody would even say that there was an operation going on here," Sanchez said.

"Typical," Richards commented.

"Nobody wants to be a snitch," Kirk said.

"There's been a couple more murders in the last couple of weeks that have the same MO. No forced entry, vic's were tied up, on their knees and shot in the head," Sanchez told the other detectives.

"Who's the big player in the game these days?" Kirk asked.

"That would be Bruce Stark."

"Stark," Kirk said and snapped his fingers a few times. "That name rings a bell."

"The Commission," Richards reminded him. Kirk chuckled a little and thought back to the day he and Richards explained the commission and its purpose to Mike Black.

"Do you know a Steven Blake or a Kevin Murdock?" Richards asked that night and handed Black their pictures.

He looked at the pictures and handed them back to Richards. "No, I don't know either of them. Should I?"

"Their street names are Cash Money and K Murder. You ever hear of them?"

"No."

"What about a guy named Stark or Billy Banner, goes by BB?" Richards continued.

"Never heard of any of them. They sound like cartoon characters to me," Black told the detective.

"Well, they've heard of you. In fact they're so worried that you're gonna kill them they formed a little group."

"What kind of group?"

"They call themselves The Commission."

"What are they, a rap group or something?"

Kirk remembered how both him and Black had gotten a good laugh at that comment. "No, they're low-rent drug dealers that used to work for Birdie," Richards said.

"Now him I've heard of. Heard they found his body in some river in Jersey," Black taunted that day. "But you answered your own question. If these guys are low-rent drug dealers, I wouldn't know them or anything about them. Maybe you should talk to Freeze. He keeps up with that kind of shit. It's like a hobby to him. But since you drove all the way out here to ask me about them, it must be something that you can only ask me."

"That would be correct," Richards said.

Then Black took a step closer to Richards and got in his face, and Kirk thought he was going to have to separate them. "You don't like me, do you, Detective Richards?" Black asked Richards. "To you, I'm just another arrogant crook who doesn't deserve the respect Kirk shows me."

"That would be correct," Richards stated plainly.

"That's why I respect you, Detective Richards, 'cause you don't like me and you have no problem lettin' me know that you don't like me. You're not like a lot of other cops who smile in my face or try to act tough. You do your job, and I respect you for that."

"Right," Richards said.

"Whatever I can do to help you, Detective Richards?"

"Somebody killed Cash Money in his apartment and K Murder was killed this weekend in a drive-by."

"I don't know anything about that. I just came back from the Bahamas today. Like I said, Freeze keeps up with that type of shit. So unless you're tellin' me that these are the guys that killed my wife, I wouldn't know anything about them. Why would I?"

"That's what I asked one of them," Richards said, referring to Bruce Stark.

"What he say?"

"He didn't have a reason either, but right now he's sitting behind fifteen guys—"

"Seventeen," Kirk corrected.

"Okay, seventeen guys; waiting for you to come after him."

"So let me get this straight," Black said. "Four baby ballers that I've never heard of, are so scared that I'm gonna kill them that they got together to protect themselves against me, but I don't know them? But now two of them are dead, which says a lot for their security, and they think it's me that killed them. So now, one of them is so scared of me that he is sittin' behind a little army waitin' on me to show up. Is that what you're tellin' me?"

By that time it was obvious that Black was fighting back his laughter and so was Kirk.

"I'm sorry, but would you mind tellin' me what my motive is for doing this?"

"See, I told you he was going to ask you that," Kirk said and dropped his head.

"I'm not out there fightin' over corners with these kids," Black said. "They play it a little too hard for me. They have no honor or loyalty; shootin' each other over bullshit. Why would I even be involved with these guys?"

After that Richards cracked a smile. "I was kinda hoping that you could tell us," he finally said. "Since they think it's all about you, I just thought I'd ask."

"It is not about me, believe that," Black told them that night.

The detectives left this latest murder scene to allow the evidence techs to do their job. On the way down the steps Sanchez told Kirk and Richards about the suspected alliance between Black, Stark and Angelo Collette. "But it's only a rumor."

"Sometimes rumors are based on fact," Richards said.

"Stark is a regular visitor at Cuisine. And him and Black seem very chummy," Sanchez said.

"But, Collette, that's the one that concerns me," Kirk said. "Him and Black are old friends and he's been trying to get a foothold in this part of the Bronx for years."

"Correct," Sanchez said. "Now, for the really big money, do you know who the last player he had in the game was?"

"Who?" Richards asked.

"One Cassandra Sims."

"Black's wife?" Richards questioned.

"The same," Sanchez confirmed.

"You don't think this is Black's work?" Richards asked.

"I don't think so," Kirk said quickly as they walked to their cars. "Unless there's something you haven't told us yet, Gene."

Sanchez shook his head. "Neither do I."

"Black has been off the grid playing legit businessman for a while now," Kirk said.

"I heard that too. And besides, these are little fish," Sanchez added. "Black takes out the top of the food chain." He got in his car and drove off.

Kirk and Richards walked to their car. "That doesn't mean we shouldn't have a talk with Stark," Richards said and got behind the wheel.

"No it doesn't."

CHAPTER TWELVE

Black and Bobby arrived at Luke's apartment and went inside. It took a while, but a woman finally came and let them in. She asked them to sit down and told them that Luke would be out in a minute. When Luke came into the room, he was on crutches and had a bandage around his thigh. His head was bandaged from the impact with the steering wheel. His arm was in a sling from getting shot in the shoulder.

"Damn," Bobby said when he saw him.

"What's up, Black? What's up, Bobby?" Luke said as he eased down in a chair.

"What happened, Luke? Who hit you?" Black asked.

"I don't know who it was. We had just left the club," Luke began.

"Who? Who's we?" Black asked.

"Me, Kenny, Duck and Ed. Me and Kenny left in one car, and Duck and Ed was in the car behind us. I looked back and saw a truck hit their car. Then a Ford 350 pulled up behind me and slammed into my rear end. I tried to get away from the truck, but it kept coming. The 350 slammed into us again. That's when I hit my head on the steering wheel."

"That's how you fucked up your head?" Bobby asked.

"Yeah," Luke said. "They ran us into a telephone pole. I got out of the car and got shot in the shoulder and caught another in my thigh. I got off a couple of shots," Luke lied. "But they went after Kenny."

"What about Ed and Duck?" Bobby asked.

"They dead too."

"But it was Kenny they wanted. They left you and went after him," Black said.

"I may not have seen who was doin' the shootin', but I know who sent them," Luke announced.

"Who?" Bobby asked.

"Cruz Villanueva."

"Who the fuck is that?" Bobby wanted to know.

"He's Hector's nephew," Black told him.

"You mean, Hector, you fucked his wife, Hector?"

"Yeah, Bobby, that Hector." Black turned to Luke. "What Cruz got to do with this?"

"Before we left the club, Kenny had words with Cruz. Whatever was said was said, and Kenny put his gun in Cruz's face."

"You know what it was about?" Black asked.

"Kenny said that Cruz was talkin' about makin' a move uptown and wanted Kenny to get down with him. But Kenny wasn't tryin' to hear that shit."

"So Cruz had him killed," Bobby said.

"That's what I think," Luke said.

"Let's go." Black stood up. "Feel better. Anything you need, you let me know."

When Black and Bobby left Luke's apartment, they went looking for Cruz. They didn't know where to find him, but Black knew somebody who might have an idea.

COMMIT TO VIOLENCE

They went to a Salsa bar off of Grand Concourse looking for Eddie Domingas. Black had known Eddie since the days when Black worked for André. Once they were inside, Black took a look around for Eddie but didn't see him.

"I could use a drink," Bobby said. He went and found a table and then a waitress brought them drinks. While they were drinking, Black saw Eddie come out of the back. Once Black was able to make eye contact with him, Eddie motioned for Black to follow him.

"I'm goin' to talk to Eddie," Black got up and followed Eddie into the men's room. When Black left the table three men walked up.

When Black walked in the men's room, Eddie was standing by the sink. The two men shook hands. Black asked him if he knew anything about what happened to Kenny. Eddie said that he hadn't heard anything about it.

"I been hearin' that Cruz is makin' noises about movin' uptown. You hear anything about that?"

"That's all it is, is talk. Cruz thinks your boy Stark is weak."

"He ain't my boy," Black said.

"The word on the street is that you stand behind him."

"Next time you hear that shit, you tell mutha fuckas that it ain't true. You know I ain't no fuckin' drug dealer, Eddie," Black told Eddie. He knew when he agreed to Angelo's proposition that this might happen.

"Whether you are or not, that's the word. I don't think Cruz will make a move."

"You know where I can find him? Just to talk."

"I'm not sure where he's livin' now, but call me tomorrow and I'll have something for you."

"Thanks, Eddie," Black said and left the men's room.

Bobby looked up and saw three men standing over him. He put his hand on his gun.

"You're Bobby Ray, ain't you?" one of the men asked.

"That's right," Bobby replied.

The three men sat down at the table.

"I don't remember askin' you to join me," Bobby said.

"That's 'cause I didn't ask."

"So who are you?" Bobby asked.

"Lex."

As soon as he said his name Bobby knew exactly who he was, and what he wanted. "Do I know you?"

"You know Ivillisa Ortiz?"

"What about her?"

"I'm surprised she never mentioned me to you," Lex said.

"I guess Ivy had other things on her mind," Bobby said and smiled.

Lex was not amused. He banged on the table. "Ivillisa is my woman—and you're gonna forget you knew her!"

Bobby held up one hand and put his gun on his lap. "Calm down, Lex. If you wanna claim her, she's all yours, kid."

"I ain't no fuckin' kid," Lex shouted and pulled out his gun.

"Everything all right?" Black asked and put the barrel of his gun to the base of Lex's skull.

Bobby brought his gun up from under the table and stood up. "Yeah, Mike, everything's fine. Lex here was just explaining that Ivillisa is his woman, and I was about to tell him that I was done with her ass anyway, so he can have her," Bobby said and came around the table. Black took Lex's gun from him and followed Bobby out.

"You know, there was a time when I would've just shot that mutha fucka and wouldn't have gave a fuck," Black said as him and Bobby got in the car.

"You're gettin' old. Shit, we both are. Back in those days, I woulda shot him as soon as he sat down and opened his mouth with that bitch shit," Bobby said and drove away. "You get anything from Eddie?"

"He says the same thing. Cruz wants to make the move uptown, but he won't 'cause he thinks we back Stark."

"I knew that shit was gonna happen. Soon as Angelo came to you with that shit, I knew this was gonna happen; whether we did shit or not."

"That's the word. We're back in the drug business."

"I wouldn't be surprised if Stark was puttin' that shit out himself," Bobby speculated. "Makes his position stronger."

"Don't you think Angelo knew that when he suggested it?"

"You probably right."

"I know I am. This is what fuckin' Angee wanted all along. 'You can be a stabilizing influence, Mikey.' I knew it was a mistake, but what could I do?"

"You couldn't tell him no; not after all the shit Angelo's done for you."

"I know."

"So what now?" Bobby asked.

"Eddie said he'd have something on where we can find Cruz tomorrow. So until then, we wait."

CHAPTER THIRTEEN

Kirk and Richards returned to the scene of the crime and began re-canvassing the building. They had been knocking on doors and then they got a break.

"I'm Detective Richards and this is Detective Kirk-land."

"What y'all want?" the woman asked. She was very slender, her eyes were prominent and her hands shook a bit.

"Can we come in?" Kirk asked.

The woman rolled her big eyes and stepped back from the door and led them into the living room. There wasn't much in the way of furniture in the small apartment. A couch, a small TV that sat on a dining room table and one chair was all there was.

"We're investigating the murders that happened in the building tonight," Richard said.

"I don't know nothin' about it," the woman said and turned up the volume on The Daily Show. "And if I did know something why would I tell you?"

Kirk pulled out a twenty-dollar bill and dropped it on the floor in front of her. "Anything you can tell us would be helpful," Richards said and laughed a little.

When the woman started to reach for the bill, Kirk put his foot on it. "I don't know who killed them boys," she said.

"What do you know?" Richards asked.

"You know who they were with?" Kirk asked.

"I heard them say they was with PR."

"PR? Who's that?"

"I don't know who he is?" she said and pulled on the twenty.

"You know where we can find this PR?" Richards asked and Kirk moved his foot.

"I don't know nothin'," she said now that she had the money.

Both detectives laughed as they left the apartment. Kirk took out his phone and called Detective Sanchez. "Gene, its Kirk. You got anything on somebody called PR? Might be the new player behind tonight's victims."

"Name isn't familiar, but I'll float it around and see what comes back."

"Thanks, Gene," Kirk said. He hung up the phone and got in the car.

"Where you wanna go now?" Richards asked.

"You call it."

"Let's go see Stark," Richards said and drove off.

According to information they had gotten from Sanchez, Stark could be found at a cafeteria-style sit down restaurant called Fat Larry's. It was a chicken and rib joint that he had taken over from a guy name Larry Mills. He kept Larry around as a front, and besides, he was a great cook; nobody made ribs like Fat Larry.

In one of their many conversations Black recommended that Stark buy or open a business. "Makes you a business man, not a drug dealer," Black told him. "And makes it a cash business."

When they arrived at the place there were a few people enjoying their meal. "Smells good," Kirk said to his partner as they entered Fat Larry's.

"What; you wanna stay and eat?"

"Maybe another time. I'll come and checkout the food," Kirk said as they approached the hostess.

"Two?" she asked.

"No," Richards said and flashed his badge. "We're looking for Bruce Stark."

The hostess picked up two menu place mats. "Follow me, please." Kirk and Richards looked at each other and then followed the hostess as she led the detectives to a table. "Can I get you something to drink?"

"No thank you," Kirk said.

"Okay, I'll let Mr. Stark know that you're here. Someone will be with you soon," she said and walked off.

When she left, Kirk got up and checked out the food behind the counter. "Food looks good too," he said as Moon approached the table.

"You detectives mind showing me your ID?" Moon asked then he looked at Kirk. "I remember you. Detective Kirkland, isn't it?"

"That's right," Kirk said and was about to show Moon his badge.

Moon held up his hand. "No need, gentlemen. Mr. Stark will be out in a minute," Moon said and walked away.

It wasn't long before Stark came and joined them at the table. "Detectives," he said and sat down.

"Nice place you got here," Kirk said.

"Thank you."

"How's business?"

"It's been a little slow lately, but hopefully it will pick up."

"How's your other business?" Richards asked.

"What other business is that, detective?"

"The business you were in the last time we talked," Richards said.

"The last time we talked, you asked me about the death of two old friends. Then you told me some ridiculous story about me being at war with Mike Black," Stark said and laughed.

"I hear you and Black are like buddies now," Richards said.

"I've met Mr. Black on several occasions since then, but I wouldn't call us buddies," Stark said.

At that point Kirk had had enough. "Let's cut the crap," he said. "We're investigating several drug murders. They were all execution style. You know anything about that?"

"No, I really don't know anything about that, detective. And since we're cuttin' the crap, if I did know something about it I *would* tell you. Mr. Black speaks very highly of you. So anything I can do to help you, detective, I'm all over it," Stark said and smiled.

"You wouldn't be going to war with anybody?" Kirk asked.

"Nah, things are all good," Stark said and they actually were. The word was getting around that Black was behind him. Kirk's visit was proof of that.

"Ever hear of a guy that goes by the name PR?" Kirk asked. "It was his people who got hit."

"No," Stark said quickly and wondered if Kirk picked up on the apprehension in his voice. "But if I hear anything I'll let you know."

Kirk stood up and handed Stark his card. "How's the food here?"

"I think it's pretty good. Larry makes the best ribs on the East Coast."

"I'll have to come back sometime and check it out."

"Any time, detective. For you,"—Stark said and looked at Richards—"it's on the house."

"I like to pay my way. But thanks for the offer."

Once they were back in the car, Richards turned to Kirk. "'Mr. Black speaks very highly of you. I'm all over it, detective.' What the fuck was that about?"

"Black thinks he owes me for clearing him on the murder beef."

"Are you kidding? He does owe you—big time. If it wasn't for you Mr. Black would be doing life right now," Richards said and drove off.

"Whatever. But I think we have an answer to one of my questions."

"Which question was that?"

"There is at least an alliance between Black and Stark. I mean just look at him. How he acted, the way he was dressed. Black's influence is written all over him. And did you notice the look on his face when I asked him about PR?"

"Yeah, he may not be involved in it, but he knows who PR is."

"So, let's go talk to Black," Kirk said.

"Like you read my mind," Richards said and headed in that direction.

When they arrived at Cuisine, Black's supper club, Lexi the informed the detectives that Mr. Black would join them shortly. Kirk and Richards took a seat at the bar and looked around for any familiar faces.

It wasn't too much longer before Lexi returned and asked the detectives to follow her. She led them to the rear of the club to Black's office. She knocked lightly and then opened the door to show the detectives in. There sat Black and Bobby.

"Detectives." Black got up and shook both of their hands. "What brings you here?"

"I came to ask you a couple of questions about a triple homicide."

Black looked at Bobby. "I'm tempted right away to say, I don't know anything about it. But go ahead, ask away," he said and offered the detectives a seat.

"You ever heard of a guy goes by the name PR?" Kirk asked.

"PR? No I haven't heard the name before. What about you, Bobby?"

"Other than every Puerto Rican in the city, you mean?" Bobby said and laughed.

"Sorry, can't help you on that one, detective. But if I do, I will let you know. What's goin' on?"

"That would be police business," Richards said.

Kirk looked at his partner. "You heard anything about some dope-boys gettin' robbed and then executed?"

"No, I haven't heard anything about that, but I'll ask around, let you know what I find out; if that wouldn't be interfering with police business, of course?" Black asked and looked at Richards.

"Pat?" Kirk asked his partner to answer.

"Go ahead and ask around," Richards said.

Black smiled. "Anything you need, I'm all over it, Kirk."

Kirk gave Black a look. "What, all you guys got the same answer?"

"I don't know what you're talkin' about."

"While we're sorta on the subject, what's the connection between you and Bruce Stark?" Kirk asked.

"You wanna know the truth?" Bobby asked quickly.

"Yes I would," Kirk said.

"I know I would," Richards chimed in.

"Idol worship," Bobby told the detectives.

"Nothing business related?" Kirk asked.

Bobby laughed. "Black and Mr. Stark don't do the same type of business."

"You of all people should know that, detective," Black said.

"Look, Kirk, the fact is that the kid worships the ground Black walks on. And that's it," Bobby said.

"How you feel about that, Black?" Richards asked.

"Personally, I think the kid should pick better role models."

"I think so too," Kirk said. "So I guess there's no truth to the rumor that you, Stark and Angelo Collette are in business together?"

Black laughed. "Where'd you hear that one?"

"I hear things in my line of work. All kinds of things. Some true, some not. But you haven't answered my question."

"No, Kirk, me and Angee have been friends for years, you know that, but we have never had any business together. And Stark, like Bobby said me and Mr. Stark don't do the same kind of business."

Kirk and Richards stood up to leave. "Right," Kirk said.

"Before you go, detective, a very good friend of mine, Kenny Lucas, was murdered in the street last night."

"Yeah, I heard about that, Black. I know you and Kenny go back some years."

"What can you tell me about it? You got any suspects?"

"Not our case, Black, sorry," Richards said and continued for the door.

"Whose case is it?"

"That would be detectives Goodson and Harris that are assigned to the case."

"Not those two assholes," Black said.

"Goodson and Harris couldn't find pussy in a ho house," Bobby said.

"Come on, Bobby, they're good cops. But at this point they have no suspects," Kirk said and followed Richards out of the office.

"You buy that?" Richards asked.

"Until something happens to show me otherwise," Kirk answered and the detectives left the restaurant.

CHAPTER FOURTEEN

Wanda Moore was the lawyer for the operation. Wanda had gotten them out of more cases than she could remember. She was as Nick once called her, "The mad scientist that made everybody rich."

"It wasn't just me, Nick. Sure, I handled the money, made some good investments, but everybody did their part. We changed with the times."

Wanda always laughed when she thought about that. Over the years she managed the money and made millions for her partners. It began early on when Wanda insisted that they start a business to run their money through. It was the same advice that Black had offered to Bruce Stark.

Wanda placed the phone back in its cradle and spun her chair around and looked out the window. She picked up the phone and dialed Nick on his cell, but got no answer—something that was happening more and more lately. Something had to give.

"You're gonna make me cum again!" Rain yelled and sat straight up on Nick. Her head drifted back and her mouth was open wide. Nick twisted her nipples. "Fuck me harder, Nick!" Rain screamed. "I'm cummin' all over your dick!"

Rain rolled off of him, grabbed his dick, lowered her head and took him into her mouth. Nick watched as Rain's tongue slide up and down his shaft. She ran circles around his head with her tongue.

"Come here and get this pussy, nigga," Rain said and got up on her hands and knees. Nick stood up and grabbed her ass. He entered her slowly, easing in inch by inch. "Don't tease me with the dick, nigga. Fuck me," Rain demanded.

He grinded his hips into Rain, spanked her ass and pushed harder. "That's it, nigga, get this pussy!" Rain began to push back and slid her hand between her legs to massage her clit. "Oh shit!" she screamed and they slammed their bodies against one another. Rain came again and Nick came right behind her.

Now that they'd had sex, Nick and Rain got ready to hit the streets again. Once Nick was dressed, he reached in his pocket and looked at his phone. He had one missed call.

"Somebody call you?" Rain asked as Nick looked at the display.

"Wanda."

"I thought I heard it buzzin' in between me screamin'," Rain said and continued to get dressed. "You gonna call her back?"

"Yeah," Nick said and walked out of the room.

"Tell her I said hello," Rain laughed.

Nick called Wanda back but there was no answer. He started to try her on her cell, but really didn't feel like getting into the reason or the lie that he would have to tell about why he didn't answer when she called. Lately, those conversations always got around to them talkin' about Rain.

Right then, Nick had much bigger issues that he knew he had to deal with. Without his knowledge, he had brought the drug business back to Black's organization at a time when they were doing everything possible, to move away from their illegal activities. He had to end this and do it before anybody, especially Black, or Wanda for that matter, got wind of it.

Rain had gotten a tip on somebody that had information on who was robbing her. They left Rain's apartment and headed for her car. To Nick's surprise, Rain stopped in front of a late model, gray Ford Taurus and Rain unlocked the door.

"When did you get this?" Nick asked and got in the car.

"This morning," Rain answered. "Too many people know my Lex on sight, and I need to keep a lower profile until we settle this shit."

"So where we goin'?"

"See a nigga named Smoke. My people tell me that he been talkin' 'bout he got connections with some niggas that's gettin' ready to do big things."

"How you know that's got anything to do with you?"

"I don't."

"Then why we goin' there?" Nick asked, questioning her logic. It was times like this when he missed Freeze. He seemed to know everybody. Freeze would always say, "Somebody know something. And they told somebody, 'cause niggas can't keep shit to themselves. All you gotta do is find the mutha fucka they told." He was usually right, and given time, he would find that person and make them tell him what he wanted to know.

"Look, you a gambler, you know more about that shit and how it works than I'll ever know. Me, I'm a drug dealer," Rain said as she drove. "That's who I am, who I always been since I was fourteen. I know how this shit go. Ain't but so many mutha fuckas can do the kind of shit this nigga was talkin' 'bout and nobody see the shit coming. They ain't talkin' 'bout some niggas from down south or Cali or Miami or some shit like that. He talkin' 'bout some local niggas raisin' up. Where they get the money? Where they gettin' the product? Could just be some nigga I ain't heard of, maybe not. But I think they makin' this move with my money and my product."

Nick couldn't argue with her logic 'cause on some level what Rain said made sense. Knowing how Rain operated, Nick checked his guns and went along for the ride, and hoped that she was right.

For the next hour and a half, they rode around from place to place trying to find out where Smoke could be found, until they got an address. When they made it to the apartment where they were told Smoke could be found, Rain stopped at the door and took out her gun. She turned to Nick. "You wanna kick it in or you want me to do it?"

Nick laughed a little and took out his gun. He kicked in the door and Rain rushed in. There were two men seated on the couch playing video games with a pile of powder cocaine on the coffee table in front of them. They started to go for their guns, but Rain fired a single shot in their direction and they froze.

While Rain held her gun on them, Nick collected their guns and checked the apartment to make sure nobody else was in there. Rain lowered her weapon.

"Which one of you is Smoke?"

"I am."

"I heard you been doin' a lot of talkin'." Rain walked up to him. "Talkin' 'bout you got connections."

"Who the fuck are you?" he said, and Rain kicked the coffee table out of her way and hit him in the mouth with her gun.

"I'm the bitch askin' the fuckin' questions," she said and held her gun to his head. "Now you gonna tell me who these niggas are you been talkin' 'bout, where they gettin' their product and where I can find them."

Smoke spit blood and smiled at Rain. "I don't know what you talkin' about."

Rain hit him again and returned her gun to his temple. "That ain't what I wanna hear. You been rollin' around tellin' mutha fuckas that you got connections with some niggas that's gettin' ready to do big things. Probably the same niggas that gave you that powder that's all over the floor now. I wanna know who these niggas are you been talkin' 'bout, where they gettin' their product and where I can find them."

"And I already told you I don't know what the fuck you talkin' about, bitch."

"Liar," Rain said and shot him in the head.

She quickly turned her gun on the other one. His eyes and mouth were wide open. "You gonna tell me what I wanna know?" Rain asked and moved her gun closer to him.

ROY GLENN

"I don't know anything about this, I swear. I just came over here to get high and play Madden," he said, shaking with his hands in the air.

"That's fucked up." Rain shot him too and walked out of the apartment. Nick shook his head and followed Rain to the car.

"That went well," Nick said sarcastically when he got in the car.

"I think so too," Rain said calmly and drove away.

Rain parked the Taurus in front of her building and got out. Nick got out of the car but instead of heading for his car, he followed Rain inside the building. They walked in silence to her apartment. Rain unlocked the door and Nick followed her in. The minute she closed and locked the door Rain began unbuckling his belt and pulling down his zipper. She dropped to her knees and took him into her mouth.

She teased his head with her tongue, and then slowly worked her way down. Rain's lips and tongue were soft and wet. As he got harder, Rain relaxed the muscles in her throat so she could take more of him into her mouth. She used the roof of her mouth to apply a little push on his shaft.

Rain licked her lips and put two fingers in her mouth and let her hands roam over her body. Her nipples were hard, so she pinched and squeezed them a little bit. It didn't take long for her pussy to start throbbing and for her hand to find its way down there. She took her fingers and spread her lips apart. Rain massaged her clit, and then slid two fingers in and out as she continued to suck. "I love your big dick."

Rain clasped her fingers together and placed them around his throbbing dick. Slowly, but ever so firmly, she moved her hands up and down. She let go with one hand and began to fondle his balls, and continued to stoke him with the other. She licked her lips and felt his dick swelling in her hand. His balls were getting fat so Rain squeezed them. Nick stood completely still and watched Rain as her tongue slide up and down his dick. With her thumb and forefinger Rain squeezed the bottom of his shaft, causing his head to swell. She ran circles around his head with her tongue, as Nick tried to reach for her. Rain moved his hands away.

Rain ran her tongue over her lips and kissed his head. In and out—deeper and deeper—she slowly took him in until she had taken almost all of him in her mouth. Nick was in ecstasy. His body became tense and rigid and Rain felt him begin to expand inside her mouth while she licked and sucked him. Rain knew he was getting ready to cum, so she squeezed it in her hand and felt it twitching.

Nick pushed away from Rain and pulled her up. He lowered his head and took her nipple between his teeth, sending an electric sensation rushing through her veins. He kissed her again, nibbled her chin, and sucked her neck. Nick forced her legs open and pinned her up against the wall. "I wanna feel that dick in me."

Nick plunged his dick into her wet pussy and stroked her hard. Rain loved it; it made her want more. Rain closed her eyes and felt herself tremble as he moved in and out of her. She bit her bottom lip to try and keep from screaming. It didn't work. "AAAAAAAHHHH!"

Rain attacked his tongue; Nick grabbed her thighs and lifted her off her feet. Before she could catch her breath, he thrust himself into her. Her eyes widened, her breath caught in her throat, her mouth was open and she her muscles began to tighten its firm grip on him.

Nick let Rain down and she led him to the bed. She pushed him down and got on top. "I'ma fuck the shit outta you, nigga. Got me cummin' like this."

Nick arched his back and pushed himself as deep and as hard into her as he could. Rain collapsed on his chest and Nick kissed her passionately until she grabbed the back of his head and forced a nipple into his mouth. Nick licked and sucked her nipple, all the while continuing to push himself inside Rain until her head drifted back with her mouth open and eyes wide, as she screamed, "I'm cummin' all over your dick!"

After Rain came she rolled off of Nick. He got out of bed and headed for the shower. "Where you goin'?"

"Home."

When he was dressed and ready to leave and said goodnight to Rain, she kissed him and lay back down. "When you see Wanda, tell her I said hello," Rain said and Nick walked out.

CHAPTER FIFTEEN

When Nick stepped into his apartment, he switched on the light and was surprised to see Wanda sitting there.

"Hi," Wanda said.

"Hi yourself. What are you doing sitting in the dark?"

"Waiting for you."

Nick walked over and sat down in the chair across from Wanda, and was glad that he'd taken a shower before he left Rain's apartment. Still he thought it was a good idea to keep his distance just in case Rain's scent lingered. "Why didn't you make yourself comfortable?"

"I wanted to talk to you."

"You can't be comfortable and talk?"

"I could have, but I didn't want to."

Nick laughed a nervous laugh. "I don't like how this is going already."

"Where were you all night?"

"I had some thing's I needed to do."

"Nobody's seen you all night or last night for that matter."

"You been checkin' up on me?"

"Don't try to turn this around, Nick. If it makes you happy to hear it, yes, Nick, yes I have been checking up on you. I want you to tell me where you've been and what you've been doing?"

"I told you, I had some business I needed to take care of," Nick said louder than he needed to.

To Wanda, it just made him sound and look guiltier than he already did. "What business, Nick? It's five-thirty in the morning. I know this business. I run the money for this business. I used to run this business!" Wanda said angrily. "So what business kept you busy until five-thirty in the morning?"

"You don't know everything that's goin' on, not any more."

"If its business I should, so why can't you just tell me what business you had that kept you busy until five-thirty in the morning?"

"Kenny got shot last night. I've been tryin' to find out who killed him."

Wanda's facial expression softened. "Kenny's dead?"

"Yes, Wanda, he was ambushed last night."

"Nobody told me about it," Wanda said.

"You know Black wants you to stay out of this part of the business."

"Still, I've known Kenny for years. Somebody should have said something to me."

"Now you know," Nick said, thinking that he had gotten out of this one.

"Okay, so you were out lookin' for Kenny's killers."

"Yes, Wanda."

"If that's all it was, why couldn't you answer your phone, or at least return my calls?"

"I told you I was busy," Nick said frustrated, knowing that Wanda was just getting started.

"Busy doin' what? If you were just ridin' around looking for whoever killed Kenny, that doesn't explain why you couldn't answer your phone or at least call me back."

Nick looked at Wanda for what seemed like a long time and thought about what to say. He thought about telling her the truth. That Rain had been dealing. That she had been robbed and several of her people had been killed, and they had been out all night looking for the shooters.

Two things prevented that: One, she wouldn't believe that's all there was to it. Mainly because it wasn't, he had just gotten finished fuckin' the shit outta Rain for the second time that night. Two, even if she did believe that was all there was to it, and he knew she wouldn't, Wanda would tell Black that Rain was dealing and that was the last thing he needed or wanted.

Nick had given Black his word that he would keep their operation drug free because of the arrangement Black had with Angelo Collette and Stark. Nick thought back to that night and how he and Black ran through hypothetical situations. At the end, they both agreed that each hypothetical always ended the same way—in jail or dead.

"I ain't goin' to jail, Nick. We already got enough problems with the DEA without this. Last thing we need right now is them crawling all over us again," Black told Nick that night.

"So what are you gonna tell Angelo?"

"I been thinking about that. How I can give Angee what he wants and without actually doin' shit."

"How you plan on doin' that?" Nick asked.

"I'm gonna get him and Stark together and then I'm gonna tell him that I would offer advise and council to Stark as a personal favor to him. But for reasons that I know he understands, I can't go any further than that."

"You think that will satisfy him?"

"As long as I can get Stark to do business and as long as I can control him. But for that to work, you gotta be my guarantee. You gotta make sure that nothing we do touches that. We can't have our hands dirty in none of that."

"I'll stay on top of it," Nick promised.

"I haven't said anything about this to Wanda. But she was there when Angelo came to Cuisine, so she knows something's up. She wasn't happy with the answer I gave her, so she'll be coming at you. But she doesn't need to know anything about this."

"Understood."

Nick knew that he couldn't tell Wanda anything about Rain or why he had to handle it, because it would lead back to the arrangement Black made with Angelo, and that wasn't what Black wanted. He had a choice to make. Remain silent and run the risk of losing Wanda. Or betray Black's confidence.

The choice was easy.

"Did whatever you were doing all night involve Rain Robinson?"

"No," Nick lied.

"Don't lie to me, Nick, please don't lie to me. Have you been with her all night?"

115

"No," Nick calmly lied again.

"Then tell me where you've been?"

Nick got up and walked toward Wanda.

"You can't tell me, can you? You can't tell me because you were with her, weren't you!" Wanda yelled.

"No!" Nick yelled back.

"Are you fucking her?" Wanda screamed.

"No!"

Wanda took a deep breath. "I don't believe you. I know you're fucking that bitch. Why can't you just be a man and tell me the truth about it."

"Why we gotta go there?" Nick said and shook his head. He never understood why Wanda thought that questioning his manhood would make him confess all of his sins.

"Because I think I deserve that much. We've known each other too long for you to think that you have to lie to me like this."

Wanda looked at Nick and waited for him to say something. When it became obvious that he wasn't, Wanda stood up and started walking toward the door.

"Where are you goin'?"

Wanda turned around. "I'm leaving, Nick, unless you give me a reason to stay."

"Stay."

"Are you fucking her?"

"No," Nick said flatly.

"Whether you are or not, and I have to be honest with you, I think you are, I don't think we need to see each other on this level anymore. Before we lose our friendship and I lose all respect for you, I should go."

Nick tried to put his arms around her.

116

"Don't, Nick. Don't do that. I can smell her on you," Wanda said and Nick backed away.

Wanda opened the door and turned to face Nick.

"Goodbye, Nick."

"Goodbye, Wanda."

"I really did love you, Nick, even though I never said it before now. I really did love you."

Wanda closed the door.

CHAPTER SIXTEEN

The sound of morning traffic woke Kirk up that next morning. He stayed at the precinct reviewing files long after Richards went home for the night. When he finally did leave the building, Kirk didn't go far. He got in his car, reclined the seat and went to sleep.

He looked at his watch. It was just after seven. After walking across the street to get a cup of coffee, Kirk went back in the building looking for Detective McNally. He had known McNally since their days at the academy and this seemed like the perfect time to catch up. Besides, McNally was vice and Kirk wanted information on the recent activities of Mike Black. It wasn't that he thought Black was involved in his case, but he couldn't rule him out either, and there was something about the rumor Sanchez mentioned about an alliance between Black, Angelo Collette and Bruce Stark that made him uneasy.

He could understand Collette hooking up with Stark; that would make sense, but what was Black's involvement? Kirk knew that Black had turned his back on the drug game years ago. But when he *was* involved, the streets ran red with blood. That was a scenario that Kirk had no desire to see again.

Kirk's fear was that his long-time friendship with Collette might be enough to bring Black in, and if that was the case, these robbery/executions may just be the beginnings of Black trying to force his way back into the market and make a statement.

"Kirk?" McNally questioned, surprised to see him when he stepped up to his desk. "What brings a high-roller like you down here?"

"Just a little information," Kirk replied and sat down.

"Tell me what you need."

"Mike Black."

Knowing Kirk's obsession with Black, McNally laughed a little. "I'm tempted to say, who?"

"Why would you say it like that, Mac?"

"'Cause the Mike Black you know doesn't exist anymore."

"That's what I keep hearing; but what about his operation?"

"Since Freeze got killed things have changed. And Black himself, the guy's completely hands off."

"So who's running the show now?"

McNally got up and walked over to his file cabinet. He pulled out a file and thumbed through it. "That's a good question, Kirk; doesn't seem like anybody is in charge."

"What about Bobby Ray?"

"Night club called Impressions. Face it, Kirk, these guys made enough money to go legit. So unless you got some new evidence on some old shit," McNally shrugged his shoulders.

"You heard anything about him and Angelo Collette?"

"Him and Collette been friends for years, never has been a business relationship, but you know all this, Kirk."

"Okay, Mac, thanks," Kirk said and left the area, but he wasn't done yet. He went back to his car and drove off.

Maybe he was going about this from the wrong angle. Or maybe he was just obsessed with pinning something on Black. He often wondered why, after making it his mission to arrest him for any of the countless murders that Kirk was sure he'd committed, when Black was in jail, he did everything in his power to clear him of murder charges in the death of his wife. Had it not been for Kirk, Black would be doing life for the crime.

Maybe the way to approach this was from the Collette side of the triangle. Kirk knew somebody that he could talk to in the organized crime division of the FBI. Kirk called and made an appointment to see him. The information he came away with was more of the same.

"Naturally, I can't go into any detail about our ongoing operations against Collette, but I can say with a high degree of certainty that there is no business between Mike Black and Collette."

"High degree, huh," Kirk said to the agent, almost sounding disappointed.

"Look, Kirk, the best I can tell you is that every once and a while, Black comes out to Collette's social club. They get pissy drunk, talk about bullshit and Black leaves."

"What about Collette and Bruce Stark?"

"Never heard of him," was the agent's answer.

Kirk still wasn't satisfied. McNally was a desk jockey, and he needed fresh info from the streets. He ran down a cop named Fields, one of McNally's detectives who was working deep cover.

As soon as Fields saw Kirk he started running, but he didn't make it too hard for Kirk to catch him, cuff him and drag him back to the car for all to see.

Once they had driven for awhile Kirk unlocked the cuffs. "What brings you to the streets, Kirk?"

"You know me; I just need a little info."

"On Mike Black I take it."

"Am I that predicable?"

"No just consistent. And Mac mentioned that you dropped by this morning askin' about Black," Fields said. "What can I do for you?"

"I'm investigating a string of drug murders, and Sanchez mentioned something about an alliance between Black, Angelo Collette and Bruce Stark. You heard anything about that?"

"All I can tell you, Kirk, is that Black is so far out of the game that it's getting boring out here. One thing I'll say for Freeze, he kept it interesting. Since Freeze got popped, they've been moving to go completely legit," Fields said. "Hey, make a left here and I'll show you what I mean."

Kirk drove down the block and Fields pointed out a storefront window.

"See that place Fast Cash?"

"Yeah, I see their commercials on TV all the time."

"Yeah, well, Black owns them. So tell me, why would he bother with the loan shark business when he can do the shit legally?"

"Okay, you convinced me," Kirk said.

When Richards got to the station, Kirk was sitting on the hood of his car in front of the building. "Isn't that what you had on yesterday?"

"Yeah."

"Did you go home at all?" Richards asked as he got behind the wheel.

"No."

"Did you at least get some sleep?"

"Yeah."

"I feel better now."

"Good. Can we go now?"

After a day of not making any progress on their case, Kirk and Richards needed something to break their way. Operating under the assumption that PR was a Hispanic male, they concentrated their efforts in those communities. They were becoming increasingly frustrated because nobody seemed to have any idea what they were talkin' about.

For the next couple of hours the detectives rolled around the city trying to get a lead on the shooters. They got a call that one of the bodies had been identified. When they got back to the station, they were informed that none of the victims had any priors. Rain made sure that most of her people were clean. She made sure none of them had a record of any kind.

The one that had been identified was reported missing by his mother; he was only sixteen years old. The detectives went to talk to the mother hoping that she might be able to identify some of the others he was found with.

When they arrived at the apartment, they were met at the door by a young woman. "Yes."

"I'm Detective Richards—"

"Yeah, I get it. Y'all the po-po. What y'all want?

"We're looking for Mrs. Betty Evans. Is she here?"

"She here. What y'all want with my mama?"

"We're investigating your brother Andrew's murder and we'd like to ask her, both of you actually, some questions," Kirk said. "May we come in?"

"Who's at the door, Seline?" came a voice from another part of the apartment.

"Po-po, mama."

"I'll be right out," Mrs. Evans said and she came in the room shortly thereafter and sat down at the table with her daughter. Kirk sat down and Richards stood behind him.

"First of all, ladies, I want to say that I'm sorry for your loss," Kirk began. "I wanted to show you some pictures of the other men he was found with."

"He wasn't no man! He was just a boy. A good boy," Mrs. Evans cried.

"Yes, ma'am, I understand."

Seline patted her mother on the shoulder to comfort her. "Mama, you just foolin' yourself. Whether you wanna admit it or not, Drew wasn't the good little boy you thought he was. Not no more, mama; hadn't been for a long time. You just didn't wanna see it."

"Don't matter. They didn't have to kill my baby."

"Like I said, I'm sorry, but I was hoping that you could help me find his killers," Kirk said and both women looked at each other. There was something about helping the police that made both of them apprehensive and just a little scared.

Kirk took pictures of all of the victims out of his jacket pocket. He slid them across the table. "Can I get you ladies to look at these pictures and tell me if you recognize any of them?"

Once again, the women looked at each other for awhile before Seline picked up the pictures. She spread them out in front of her and they both looked at them. Mrs. Evans sat back and looked away.

"These two," Seline said and pointed at two of the pictures. "They been here to pick him up a few times."

"You wouldn't happen to know what their names are?"

"No. I didn't want to know nothing about what he was doing," she said and shed a tear.

"Did you ever hear your brother or these other two mention somebody named PR?"

"He said PR was gonna put him on top."

"Nothing else? Who he is; where we can find him?"

"Nope. Just that they was makin' stupid money at their spot."

"I can't listen to this," Mrs. Evans jumped up and said. She went very quickly back to her room and slammed the door.

"She in denial for real about Drew. Since his daddy left she been doing the best she can, but with her being gone all night workin' for years, she didn't know what he turned into."

Kirk got up from the table. He gave Seline a card. "If you have anything else, or need anything, please let me know." Kirk and Richards left the apartment and went back to looking for PR.

Then they got a call about another possible rob-
bery/execution. "That's all we need," Richards said.
"Another case we got no leads on."

"It's strange that not even the usual more talkative
people have the slightest idea what we're talking about.
Maybe our assumption that our mystery player is Puerto
Rican or even Hispanic, is wrong."

"But it was at least worth a shot. I mean it was so obvious," Richards said.

"And maybe that was by design. Whoever it is wants
to keep their name off the street."

"A baller who doesn't want street cred?"

"If that's true, where does that leave us, Pat?"

"Walking through this thing blind as bats."

"As much as I hate to admit it, you're right. So let's
look at what we got."

"Okay. We got bodies. All tied up, all shot in the
head—executed. Those are the hard facts. Beyond that,
what we got is that we assume they were executed dur-
ing a drug robbery. We got a crack head who gave us the
name PR. That was confirmed by the Evans girl. But so
far, finding him hasn't turned out to be shit."

"You're right. Other than the bodies, all we got are a
bunch of assumptions," Kirk said.

"So what we got is zip," Richards added.

When they got to the apartment they found detectives
Goodson and Harris standing in the hallway. "Not these
two assholes," Kirk said to Richards.

"Hey, what was that you told Black; they're good
cops."

"I was lying. Bobby was right, they couldn't find pussy in a ho house."

Richards laughed. "Be nice."

"I am," Kirk said.

It wasn't that they were bad cops; they were just more than willing to take the shortest, easiest route to closing a case. And if that meant dumping a tough case on some other detective, they wouldn't hesitate.

First thing Kirk noticed as they approached the door was that it appeared to be kicked in. In each of the cases there were no signs of forced entry, which suggested that the shooters were allowed to enter. Either because they knew them, or they were expecting to do business.

Kirk pointed the door out to Richards. Harris started trying to push the case off on them as soon as they were close enough to hear. "I know you guys been workin' these drug-related robbery murders. I think this might be another one."

"Tech's been here yet?" Kirk asked.

"Not yet; busy day. Reyes and his team are on their way," Goodson said.

"Pat."

Richards went in the apartment while Kirk stayed in the hallway with Goodson and Harris. Not that he thought they would leave, but there was no point running the risk. Besides, since the CSI team hadn't been there, he didn't want to take the chance of inadvertently disturbing what might be evidence. The fewer people entering the crime scene, the better.

Five minutes later, Richards came out. "What you got, Pat?"

"Two black males; both shot in the head."

"Just like your other cases, right?" Harris said.

"Wrong." Richards turned to Kirk. "Other than the fact that they were shot in the head, the similarity ends there."

"What makes you say that?" Goodson asked.

"The victims were shot while sitting on the couch. Not on their knees like the others. Their hands weren't tied behind their backs. Oh yeah, there's at least an eighth of coke on the floor, probably from the coffee table that was turned over next to it. Near as I can tell, those guys were playing video games and getting zooted when somebody kicked in the door, turned over the table and shot them in the head."

"Sounds like there is no connection to our case at all," Kirk said and started walking down the hall.

"Sorry. Guess you'll have to put in some work on this one," Richards said and followed Kirk down the hall.

"Got anything on the Lucas case yet?" Kirk asked as he walked.

"Nothing but dead ends," Harris shouted back.

"Yeah, but we're on top of it," Goodson said and laughed as he entered the apartment.

CHAPTER SEVENTEEN

Black received a call on Bobby's phone from Eddie Domingas, letting him know that Cruz Villanueva was having dinner at La Caridad Restaurant on West Kingsbridge Road. When the call came Black, along with Bobby and Wanda were at a meeting with their financial advisor, Meka Brazil. She was discussing offshore investment possibilities for the group to consider.

"There's a company that makes multimedia switching gear for cable companies that recently received certification for its Safari C3 product line in Russia, through the Ministry of Communications."

"That sounds promising," Wanda said.

"It has the potential to be. Especially when you consider Eastern Europe has a ways to go in terms of communications infrastructure to catch up with the rest of the world, any long-term investment represents a significant opportunity," Meka said. "Then there's wind."

"Wind?" Bobby asked.

"The United States, Russia and Canada have the greatest capacity for wind power. In the Kola Peninsula in the Murmansk region. The problem is that a lot of the area available for wind power in Russia is far from major cities. As the business capability in the region improves and construction of new transmission lines moves forward, those companies can begin servicing some of the major cities. "

"It's something for us to think about," Black said. That's when Eddie called and Black and Bobby left.

When they got to La Caridad they spotted Cruz seated at a table with another man and two women, having dinner.

"That's him. Come on," Black said, and he and Bobby started for Cruz. As they got closer a man stepped out to block their path. "Where you think you're going?"

"Over there," Black said and pointed at Cruz.

The man put his hand on Black's chest to stop him. "Nobody goes back there," he said.

"Okay." Black grabbed the man's arm then twisted it behind his back. Black tightened his grip. "You tell Cruz that Mike Black and Bobby Ray would like a few minutes of his time," Black said and let go of the man's arm and pushed him toward Cruz.

The man walked away shaking his arm as he went. He went to Cruz's table and whispered in his ear. When he pointed in their direction, Cruz looked up and saw Black and Bobby standing there.

"Shit," Cruz said and leaned close to his partner Jorge. "What the fuck they doin' here?"

"I don't know," Jorge said.

"Let them come," Cruz said, and the man went to get Black and Bobby. When he got close to them he signaled for them to follow him.

Cruz saw them coming. "Stay close," he said to Jorge, and he and the women got up from the table.

"Hello, ladies," Bobby said to them as they passed. Both ladies smiled and kept walking.

Black and Bobby got to the table just as the busboy came to clear it. Black and Cruz looked at one another. No one moved or said a word as the busboy did his work. When he was finished and left the table, Black and Bobby sat down. Jorge stood next to the table.

"Mike Black and Bobby Ray, huh? My Uncle Hector used to talk about you guys all the time," Cruz said.

"How is Uncle Hector?" Bobby asked.

"He's doin' good. My uncle is a great man."

"How's your Aunt Nina?" Black asked.

Cruz looked at Black. "She's good, too."

"You tell her I asked for her," Black said and thought about the last time he saw Nina. It was right after Shy was kidnapped in the Bahamas. The kidnappers left the island by boat and headed for Miami.

When Black, along with Bobby and Nick, got to Miami, he stopped at La Covacha to ask Hector if he knew anything about the kidnapping. They checked inside and then went out on the patio, but Hector wasn't out there so they went back inside. That's when Black saw Nina coming out of the VIP room and make her way to the bar. Black walked up behind her.

"Hello, Nina."

Nina closed her eyes and her head drifted back at the sound of his voice. "Hello, Black," she said without looking at him. "What are you doing here?"

"I'm looking for Hector."

"I was hoping you'd say something noble like you came here looking for me; that you couldn't live another minute without seeing me."

"It is good to see you, Nina, even if you won't look at me." Nina took a deep breath and turned around slowly. "You look good, Nina."

"So do you. Very good."

"Where's Hector?" Black asked quickly before he took the conversation in another direction.

"He's in the VIP room. But if you stand here and talk to me long enough, he'll be out here soon. I'm sure somebody will run and tell him that I'm out here talking to this big, fine black man," Nina said and put her hand on Black's chest.

"I wanna *talk* to him, Nina," Black said and very slowly removed her hand from his chest. "Not have to kill him over you."

Nina looked at the ring on Black's finger. "You're married?"

"Happily."

"Now that we're both married, maybe you'll come down here to see me."

"I still don't mess with married women."

"Is that why you never came looking for me?"

"It's the only reason I didn't come and get you, Nina. If you weren't married to Hector," Black paused and looked around the club. "Who knows?"

"I do." Nina smiled a satisfied smile and turned around to motion for a waitress. When one responded Nina talked to her for a minute, then she returned her attention to Black. "Tell her what you want."

Black reached in his pocket and handed the woman a hundred dollar bill. "Tell Mr. Villanueva that Mike Black sends his respect and asks that Mr. Villanueva give him a minute of his time. Tell him exactly what I said. I'll be right here waiting for his answer."

The waitress was about to go deliver the message, but Nina stopped her. "Wait until ten minutes after I'm back in the VIP room before you come in there." Once the waitress was gone, Nina turned to Black. "Goodbye, Black. I want to kiss you. I want you to hold me in your arms and kiss me. Not just a goodbye kiss or a hug and a kiss on the cheek. I want you to kiss me the way that you used to." Nina took a step closer and ran her hand up Black's crotch. Then Nina whispered in his ear, "What I'd really like to do is suck that big dick and then ride you until I feel it swell up and explode inside me." And then Nina stepped away. "But then somebody would die tonight. Goodbye, Mike Black. I hope this won't be the last time I see you."

"You never know, Nina. Anything is possible."

"We'll see," Nina said and walked toward the VIP room. It was a half-hour later when Black looked up and saw two men escorting Nina out of the VIP room and out of the club.

Hector didn't know anything about Shy's kidnapping so Black left the club. He really didn't think that Hector knew anything about it but, "You never know when we might need an ally down here. Let's get back to New York. And besides," Black paused as Bobby drove off. "I really came here to see Nina."

Cruz looked angrily at Black. He had heard the whisperings at family gatherings about his favorite Aunt Nina and Mike Black, and the reason Hector sent her to Miami a year before he actually made his move down there himself.

Even though Hector spoke of Black with respect now, and told Cruz not to fuck with Black, he was anxious to take him on. He thought that it was disrespectful for Black to even mention Nina's name in front of him. It just made Cruz more determined to prove something to his uncle and prove it against Black.

"Can I get you a drink?"

"I'm particular about who I drink with," Bobby said and smiled at Cruz.

Cruz looked up at Jorge. "What can I do for you, Black?" he asked.

Black leaned forward. "I hear a lot of things but I don't pay very much attention to them."

"Why is that?" Cruz asked.

"'Cause a lot of men talk, but it's what they do that impresses me."

"What you heard?"

"Like I said, it doesn't matter. 'Cause until that talk becomes action, it's all just talk. But what I do wanna ask you about is Kenny Lucas."

"I heard he got popped," Cruz said and laughed a little. Bobby started to reach for his gun, but Black grabbed his hand.

"What were you and Kenny beefin' about that night at the club?"

"You got it all wrong. Me and Kenny wasn't beefin' 'bout nothin'."

"Then what was his gun doin' in your face?" Bobby asked.

"What you tryin' to say? You tryin' to say that I killed him?" Cruz shouted.

"The thought occurred to me," Black said.

Cruz sprung to his feet. "If I killed him, I ain't got no problem sayin' I did it. 'Cause I represent mine."

As Cruz's men began to move closer around the table, Black looked at Bobby and then back to Cruz. Bobby turned over the table and Black stood up with both of his guns drawn.

Cruz fell over his chair.

Black stepped up quickly and stood over him. "And I ain't got no problem with killin' you right now," Black said.

Cruz put up his hands. "I got no problem with you, Black. And I ain't kill your boy."

"That's all I wanted to know," Black said, and he and Bobby backed out of La Caridad. Jorge stepped to the table and tried to help Cruz get up. "You okay?" he asked with his hand out.

Cruz slapped his hand away and got to his feet. He watched Black and Bobby leave. "I'm gonna kill that mutha fucka."

"But your uncle said to leave Black alone," Jorge reminded Cruz.

Cruz got in Jorge's face. "I don't give a fuck what my uncle says. That bitch is gonna die. And I'm gonna be the one to kill him."

After leaving La Caridad, Black went to Cynt's to pick up his car. He had an appointment to meet Jada West at her apartment in midtown. On the way there, Bobby asked, "Do you believe him?"

"I don't know, Bobby. He might've had him killed. He might know about it. Either way, we gonna have to deal with it."

"Any time we get too comfortable, somebody always comes along to try us."

"And we'll kill them, too," Black said and thought about the natural order of things as they arrived at Cynt's.

"So where you say you had to go?" Bobby asked.

"I'm going to meet Jada West. She said she had something important to talk to me about. You should ride. You might need her services."

"I got something that I need to take care of. And besides, her ho's charge too fuckin' much; a thousand dollars for some pussy? No fuckin' thank you. But with all this shit goin' on, I'd feel better if you took somebody with you," Bobby said.

"I'll be fine," Black said, but he knew Bobby was right. He looked around the room. "I'll take Victor."

Black walked up to Victor, who was being entertained by two dancers. "You doin' anything right now?" Black asked.

"No."

Black threw Victor the keys to his car. "Now you are. Come on."

CHAPTER EIGHTEEN

Nick hadn't slept much that day, and what little sleep he got was haunted by dreams of Wanda walking out on him. Her last words to him before she left his apartment that morning rang in his ears. "I really did love you, Nick, even though I never said it before now. I really did love you."

Although he always believed that Wanda loved him, there were times when he would have given anything to hear her say it. It hurt for those to be her last words. It felt like Wanda had stuck a knife in his gut and turned it. He felt bad about what he had done to Wanda, and at the same time, he didn't feel bad about what he was doing with Rain. He didn't feel for Rain the way he felt for Wanda, but there was something about Rain; something that made her and her sex irresistible.

Nick rolled out of bed and got ready to make his rounds. When he left his apartment, he got as far as Cynt's. He sat down at the bar. "Johnny Black, and leave the bottle," Nick said and the bartender did as she was told. At one point Cynt tried to talk to him, but gave up when she got no answer to the question, "What's bothering you?"

He knew that Cynt would hear about it sooner or later. He didn't want her sympathy or her condemnation when he explained that Wanda had left him because he was fucking Rain.

While Nick was trying to drown his sorrows in Johnny Black, Bobby was at Cynt's too. He came out of the back with one of the dancers on his arm. He handed her a bill and was about to leave when he saw Nick sitting at the bar.

Bobby walked over to him and sat down. "What's up, Nick?"

"What's up, Bobby," Nick said and drained his glass.

Bobby looked at him and then at the bottle. Nick picked up the bottle and poured himself another drink. Bobby signaled for the bartender to bring him a glass.

"Mind if I join you?" Bobby asked.

"Go ahead." Nick said. Bobby poured himself a drink and filled Nick's glass. "What you doin' here?" Nick asked.

"Gettin' my dick sucked," Bobby said.

The two of them sat drinking in silence. Every now and then, Bobby would look around at the array of naked women dancing around the club. He knew all of them and had fucked most of them. Some came over and spoke, others just waved. One or two tried to make conversation, but Bobby quickly dismissed them. He picked up the bottle and poured him another. Then he refreshed Nick's drink.

They sat quietly drinking through two more rounds before Bobby said something to Nick. "Something bothering you?"

"What makes you ask?" Nick replied and turned up his drink. He poured the last of the bottle into his glass. Bobby signaled for the bartender to bring another bottle. The bartender cracked the bottle open and poured Bobby another shot. By that time Nick had crushed his, and held out his glass for another.

"You drinkin' like a man that got something on his mind that he doesn't wanna deal with. When shit like that happens to me, I just say fuck it."

"Fuck it?"

"Yeah, fuck it."

"All right then," Nick said and raised his glass. "Fuck it." They both turned up their glasses and drained them.

"Now, don't you feel better?"

"No."

"That's because you didn't mean it when you said it. See, for it to work you gotta say it and know that whatever it is that's fuckin' with you is something that you got no control over, for whatever reason, and then you say fuck it and put it behind you," Bobby said.

Nick looked at Bobby and shook his head. "Me and Wanda broke up."

"Oh."

"Yeah," Nick said poured another.

"What. She find out about you and Rain?"

"Yeah."

"Yeah, well, that shit was bound to happen sooner of later."

"Was it?"

"Yeah, Nick, it was. I mean it ain't like you were tryin' real hard to keep that shit a secret. Too many mutha fuckas knew about it and some of those that did, talk to

Wanda. Shit, Rain's ass would say in a heartbeat that you were her man and that bitch Wanda can't do shit to stop it."

"She did?"

"Heard her say that shit myself."

"I guess you're right, so fuck it. Did I say it right?"

"Fuck you, Nick. The fact is that you ain't the first nigga to get caught up with a good pussy havin' young girl. The shit happened to me," Bobby said and thought about his relationship with Cat.

She was barely twenty-two and fine as hell. "Nice size titties, little-bitty waist, with a toot-booty that can stop traffic," Bobby told Nick. That body made her one of the most popular dancers at Cynt's until she got fired for being late or not showing up at all.

It began while Black was living in the Bahamas and Wanda was losing her mind about Freeze letting things get rundown at Cuisine, and gettin' sloppy with every-thing else. One night while Bobby was at Cynt's check-ing up on Freeze, he introduced him to Cat and she danced for Bobby. "Damn that bitch could dance and she was cool. I wasn't even tryin' to fuck her. We would just hangout; talk shit, that's it."

Nick thought back to the way things began with him and Rain. At the time he had no intention of fucking her. In fact, he didn't even like her. But it happened an-yway.

Bobby told Nick that after a while things with Cat be-gan getting out of control. The longer it went on the more Cat was making it hard on his marriage to Pam. It had gotten to the point that Cat was calling the house and talking to Pam.

"After Cat made herself known to Pam and she did what she did to end it, I figured out the there wasn't any woman worth losing Pam over."

"So what you doin' here gettin' your dick sucked?"

"I don't know if you know this, but Pam and I don't have sex anymore."

"I didn't know that? I mean I heard you say that Pam understands that if she isn't gonna give you any pussy that somebody is, but I thought it was just some shit you was tellin' Wanda to get her off your back."

"Nope. She feels like she can be a good wife and mother to our children, but Pam doesn't feel like she can bring herself to have sex with me after what happened. Things really got wild with Cat. That's why I come here, get what I came to get and go home. I ain't got no feelings for none of these ho's and they ain't got none for me. And I like it that way. They're just a place to bust a nut in. I get what I want, they get what they want," Bobby said. He didn't think that Nick needed to know that Pam wanted a divorce because of his relationship with Ivillisa Ortiz.

"Simple."

"This way nobody gets hurt, 'cause nobody's feelings are involved. I let Cat get off-the-chain, just like you doin' with Rain."

"I see that now."

"Mind if I ask you a question?"

"Go ahead?"

"I always wondered what the attraction was. I hope you don't get mad behind me sayin' this, I know she got body for days, but Rain ain't the prettiest mutha fucka in world."

140

Nick laughed a little and shrugged his shoulders. "She ain't, is she?"

"No she ain't."

"There's more to Rain than just her looks. I like being around her for some reason."

"Want me to tell you why?"

"Yeah, go ahead."

"I see how Rain carries it. She is all gangster; all the time."

"Damn sure is."

"That's part of why you like being around her," Bobby said and Nick didn't quite get it. "When I used to hang out with Cat, it wasn't like being with Pam. Cat was funny, she talked big shit and would do wild shit just for the fun of it."

"She was everything that Pam isn't."

"Exactly. And if you had to find a woman who was the exact opposite of Wanda, Rain is definitely the one."

"I see your point," Nick said and poured another drink.

"I wouldn't worry too much about that shit, Nick. Shit will work itself out and Wanda will be back," Bobby said and had another drink.

"I don't think so, Bobby."

"Why not?"

"There's more to it than just me fuckin' Rain."

"What else?"

"Without me knowing it, Rain has been dealin'."

"That's not good. Mike know about that?"

"You tell me?"

"Far as I know he don't. We been too busy with business."

141

"Now somebody's been robbin' and killin' her dealers. So the last couple of days I been with her tryin' to find out who it is and squash it before it goes any further. But Wanda was lookin' for me and wanted to know where I'd been the last few days."

"Damn."

"Even if she believed I wasn't fuckin' her, if I told Wanda what I've been doin'—"

"She'd tell Mike about Rain and you don't want that."

"Especially now that we got this arrangement with Angelo and Stark. And to make matters worse, I think she's buyin' from Stark."

Bobby grabbed the bottle. "I see why you're sittin' here gettin' fucked up." He poured himself a drink.

"Good, I'm glad you understand." Nick took the bottle from Bobby and poured himself another drink.

"What you gonna do?"

"Bobby, I don't know. But whatever I do it won't be today."

"Whatever you decide to do, if you need me for anything, I'm there for you," Bobby said and raised his glass.

"Thanks Bobby. That means a lot."

CHAPTER NINETEEN

Black and Victor were on their way to the apartment of Jada West. In a very short time, Ms. West was running one of the top escort services in the city.

It began when she was working a job at a market research company, scrambling for money, and dodging the landlord. Jada's life began to change when she stopped to pick up a two-piece snack from Fat Larry's, and she stopped to admire a royal blue drop-top Beamer with baby blue leather and wood panel interior. Jada wondered if she'd ever see the day when she could afford shit like that.

"Jada, that you girl?" the driver asked.

When she snatched off her shades and pulled her hat's brim back, Jada's mouth dropped. "Diane?"

Diane and Jada worked together at the marketing company for nearly a year. "You ain't gonna make any real money punchin' no damn clock. I can tell you that much for sure. Are you ready to make some real paper?" she asked.

"Girl, you just don't know," Jada said.

"I dance at this little club called Ecstasy on Friday and Saturday nights," she said calmly. "Say what you want, but I never leave with any less than five hundred dollars a night," Diane said. Jada let the figure roll around in her head. For two night's worth of work, Diane made one thousand dollars? That's almost triple what Jada made for working eighty hours.

"I don't know, Diane. I just don't think I could do that in front of a bunch of horny men."

"I'm tellin' you, you could make a grip. You got a bomb-ass body too. Them titties and that ass, I'm tellin' you, girl, you sleepin' on your best money makers!"

After three weeks at Ecstasy, Jada became Miss Kitty. She waltzed out on stage dressed in a short, tight leather miniskirt with a garter belt, black fishnet stockings, black leather bra, and a long pair of black gloves. The final touch was a small and elegant silk mask. Within two months time, Miss Kitty had her own small but generous following.

Jada was invited to dance at a private party for a rapper called The One. It was the night that changed her life forever. Later that night, Jada was introduced to The One. "You a bad mutha fucka, you know that?" The One said to Jada.

"Thank you," she purred modestly.

"I wanna fuck you."

"It'll cost you," Jada said.

"You ain't said shit to me, mommy," The One said. "Why don't I double what you usually charge? I always gets what I want."

Jada thought The One was fine as hell, but since she wasn't plannin' on fuckin' him or anybody else in there, she decided to get ridiculous. "Two grand," Jada said quickly, thinking that he would say she was crazy.

"Why don't we make it three," The One said and her eyes lit up. Jada saw herself as a dancer and an entertainer, not a ho. Most of the other dancers were letting drunk-ass niggas fuck them cheap. Jada had taken pride in the fact that she wasn't that kind of dancer. But three grand just to fuck him, Jada knew that she couldn't turn down that kind of money.

When it was over, and it didn't last very long, Jada felt used. *Probably because I have been used,* Jada thought on her way to the elevator. But at the same time, she was smiling inside at the money she'd just made in less than five minutes, and Jada wondered who really used who. She began to think about how easy that actually was as opposed to what she was doing dancing at the club. She knew if she busted her ass and hustled all night, she could make a grand, maybe more on a good night. But Jada had just made three times that amount and barely broke a sweat.

When the elevator stopped on the twenty-sixth floor, a woman stepped into the elevator. "My name is Sasha Deverox." When Sasha told Jada that she was an escort, Jada knew Sasha was somebody she needed to get to know better. The way she was dressed, the way she carried herself, Jada knew being an escort was a much better hustle than stripping.

Sasha offered to let Jada work under her until she felt comfortable going out on her own. Under Sasha's tutelage Jada learned how to walk, talk and dress like a lady. When that day came for Jada to go out on her own, she met with Sasha. "You think you're ready to fly solo? Is that what you think you wanna tell me?"

"I think I'm ready. No, I know I'm ready."

"Look at you, Jada. All dressed up tryin' to be a lady. Do you remember who you were when I met you? You couldn't talk, you could barely walk without falling on your face, and you definitely had the most ghetto taste in clothes," Sasha laughed and Jada wanted to kick her ass. "I made you," Sasha leaned forward and said sternly. "It was me who taught you how to walk without falling; how to talk without having to end every sentence with a cuss word. And it was me who taught you how to dress like a lady. I taught you all those things. If it wasn't for me, you'd still be shakin' your ass at that dive. I made you, Jada," she said again, but this time she stuck her finger in Jada's face. "Never forget that."

"No, Sasha," Jada said to her. "I won't forget any of that." Although she hated to admit it, Sasha was absolutely right about her.

Then Sasha smiled. "Stop looking like that." Her smile turned into laughter. "I was just playing with you. Listen, honey, I am so proud of you and the way you handle yourself now. Jada, you have come so far. You've been ready to fly solo for a long time."

Sasha was Jada's madam. Even though she hated the word, she was her pimp. That's where the money was, not laying on her back with her legs in the air. Jada was giving Sasha two, sometimes three grand a week. "If I were to get a couple of girls working for me, I could pull in five, six grand a week."

From there, Jada put together her team: Diane, Bella and Simone. Their target group was the new rich—the ones who just stumbled into money—the ones who don't quite know how to act now that they had it.

"Ballers," Diane said.

"I'm talking about music industry insiders, rappers, music producers, actors, movie and television producers, and of course ballers," Jada told her new team. And from there Jada West worked her way to the top.

It was 8:00 P.M. sharp when Black and Victor arrived at Jada's apartment. They went up in the elevator and Black rang the bell.

"What do you want me to do?" Victor asked.

"You wait here. Make sure nobody comes in on me," Black said.

"Just stand here; that's it?"

"That's it," Black said as Jada opened the door. As she always did every time he saw her, Jada looked phenomenal. She was dressed in a black Herve Leger armor trim dress with a single strap across the shoulder and a string of pearls.

"Good evening, Mr. Black," Jada said and smiled.

"Good evening, Ms. West."

"Please come in," she said and stepped to the side to let him pass.

Black walked in the apartment and looked around. "Very nice place you have here, Ms. West."

"Thank you, Mr. Black. Please have a seat. Can I get you something to drink?"

"Thank you," Black said and watched Jada as she walked toward the bar to fix his drink. He liked Jada—admired her style. Aside from being one of the most beautiful women he had ever met, Jada West had class.

Jada returned with his drink and sat down next to him. "Rémy Martin VSOP, right?"

"You remembered. I cannot help but be touched. But in your business, I'm sure little things like that are part of the job," Black said and Jada smiled.

"That's true, but I think it's more than that. I want to remember the things that are important to you."

"So what I drink is important to you?"

"You're a very important man, Mr. Black. For more reasons than just business. Everything about you is important to me."

"You flatter me, Ms. West."

"You don't have to be so formal, Mr. Black, you can call me Jada."

"Why don't I just call you Miss Kitty," Black said.

Jada giggled and as she usually did, Black enjoyed the sound of it and the smile that came with. "Nobody has called me that in years," she said and thought back to the night she met Black. It was the same night she met The One.

Black was sitting at a table in the corner with the club's manager, Bruce-Bruce, when he caught Jada's eye. She was just about to make her way over there when she was surrounded by three men hollering, "Miss Kitty, Miss Kitty," and dropping money at her feet. Without taking her eyes off Black, Jada took off her outfit and went to work. When the song ended, Jada picked up her money and went back to the dressing room.

When she returned to the floor, Jada looked around the club for Black, but she didn't see him. Jada was startled when a deep and sexy voice said, "Miss Kitty, right?"

"That's me."

"I enjoyed watching you dance," Black said.

"Thanks. You a friend of Bruce-Bruce?"

"I guess you could say that."

"I haven't seen you here before, so I guess you're part of The One's entourage."

Jada remembered that Black flashed a smile and she got wet. "Not exactly. I own the company that manages The One."

"Oh really," Jada said, knowing that Black was somebody she needed to know. They talked for a minute after that, and then Black left the party.

Black looked at Jada and smiled. It had the same effect on her that it had the first time. Her mind began to drift but she caught herself. She had important business to discuss with Black. When her issues were behind her, then she could think about indulging her passion. "No, Mr. Black, I think I'd prefer it if you called me Jada. I left Miss Kitty back at the club years ago."

"Okay, Jada it is, but only if you call me Mike."

"I'd like that," Jada smiled and Black thought about how much he wanted to strip her out of that Herve Leger black dress and bend her over the closet piece of furniture, but he remembered that she invited him there to talk business.

Black took a sip of his drink. "So, tell me, Jada, what did you want to see me about?"

"I have a problem that I need your help with," Jada began.

"What can I do for you?"

"You see, there's this guy that's trying to shake me down."

"What do you mean, tryin' to shake you down?" Black asked even though he had a good idea.

"It began about a month ago. One of my girls was out with a client. After they had sex and she got ready to leave, he beat her up."

"Was she hurt badly?" Black asked and finished his drink.

"Bad enough that she couldn't work for a couple of weeks until her wounds healed. A week later the same thing happened again. Same pattern, new client, took the girl someplace secluded, beat her after sex," Jada said and took Black's glass from his hand. She went to the bar to refresh his drink. "A few days later I was at The Pen-Top Bar & Terrace inside the Peninsula Hotel having dinner with a potential client, when this man sits down at the table with us," Jada said as she poured.

"What did he want?"

"Once he scared off the client, he told me that he was my new partner," Jada returned with the drink and handed it to Black. "He said that he was responsible for what had happened to my girls, and if I wanted it to stop that I would give him twenty percent."

"What did you tell him?"

Jada laughed. "I basically told him to kiss my ass, and I got up and left."

"Since we're having this conversation, I take it that it didn't stop there."

"No. I figured if we tightened up and did a better job of screening our clients that at least the girls would be safe, and I would deal with this clown and his threats. But then he began catching them before they got to the clients or after they were finished."

"Your girls don't have security?"

"Some do. They have men that drive them to their appointments and pick them up afterwards, but he targeted the ones that don't have any type of security. He came here last night and caught me in the elevator."

"He didn't hurt you did he?"

"No. He just wanted to make his point and scare me."

"What he say?"

"Same thing; my problems go away for twenty percent."

"Don't you have security?"

"No."

"Maybe you should get some," Black advised.

"No," Jada insisted. "I don't need security. I need Mike Black," she said and moved close to him.

"Me? Why you think you need me?"

"Do I really need to answer that question?"

"No. Not really. I get the point. So, if take care of this guy for you, what makes you think that I wouldn't want twenty percent of your business?"

"Because you'd be doing me a favor. You know, like the one I did for you not too long ago."

"I see."

"I was talking to James Fremeno. You remember the reporter from the New York Post that I set out for you."

"How's he doing?"

"He said that he wanted to thank me for putting him in touch with Miss Collins, because the story she gave him was inline to win some award for reporting."

"The Tom Renner Award for Crime Reporting."

"Was that what it was?" Jada giggled. "Then he told me that the guy the articles were about ended up getting murdered in Mexico. A DEA agent; Peter J. Vinnelli, I believe his name was."

"I see you've been checkin' up on me, Ms. West?"

"Jada, please, call me Jada," she said and smiled at Black. "But, no, I'm not checking up on you. It's like I told you, you're a very important man, Mike Black. And I try to know important things about important men."

"How do you wanna come outta this?"

"With this guy off my back and me not owing you twenty percent of my business," Jada said quietly.

"How'd you leave it with him?"

"He said he would be back here tomorrow afternoon, and he'll expect my answer."

"What time tomorrow?"

"He didn't say."

Black looked at Jada for what seemed to her like a long time. "Okay. I'll see what I can do for you."

"That's the best I could ask for," Jada said.

"What's this guy's name?"

"He said his name was Mushnikov. I think that's how it's pronounced."

"Oleg Mushnikov?" Black asked.

"I believe so. Do you know him?"

"Yeah, I know Oleg. We're not exactly what you'd call friends, but I do know him," Black said and laughed a little. "You mind if I use your phone?"

"Not at all," Jada said and got up to get it. She knew she had come to the right person. Jada always loved a man who could get things done for her, and Mike Black was that type of man.

She handed Black the phone and he dialed a number. "Yeah," a man's voice answered.

152

"Let me speak to Angelo."

"Who the fuck is this?"

"Mike Black."

"Who the fuck is that?"

"I'm the mutha fucka that's gonna put a bullet in your brain if you don't put Angee on the phone right fuckin' now!" Black shouted and looked at Jada. He put his hand over the phone. "Please, excuse my language," he said softly and returned his attention to the phone. He could hear Angelo in the background asking who was on the phone.

"Some guy says his name is Mike Black."

"Give me the phone, fuckin' moron," Angelo said. "Mikey! How's it goin'?"

"Everything's good, Angee. What about you?"

"Same old shit. You on your way out here? I got a bottle of Rémy Martin XO Premier Cru here with your name on it."

"Not tonight, Angee, I got a couple of things goin' right now, but I need your help with something."

"What's up?"

"When's the last time you talked to Oleg?"

"It's been a minute. Probably the last time we all got drunk together, why?"

"I need to talk to him. Can you arrange a sit down with him?"

"Sure. I'll give him a call in the morning," Angelo said.

"No, Angee, I need to talk to him tonight," Black said and looked at Jada. "Can you do it?"

"Sounds serious."

"Yeah, Angee, it kinda is." Jada smiled at him and pushed her pouty lips out a little.

"I'll give him a call right now and get back to you."

"Thanks, Angee," Black said and ended the call. He turned to Jada and handed her the phone. "I'll take Oleg off your back, and then we'll talk about what you owe me, Ms. West," he said and stood up.

"Jada, please, Jada," she said and walked Black to the door. "And thank you for agreeing to help me," Jada said and kissed Black on the cheek.

"What was that for?"

"Just wanted to see how it felt," Jada said.

"And?"

Jada opened the door. "We'll talk about that when you tell me what I owe you."

"Fair enough," Black said and left her apartment and walked past Victor. "Come on, we got shit to do."

CHAPTER TWENTY

After leaving Jada's apartment, Black called Bobby's cell phone and it went straight to voicemail.

"That's unusual," Black said and dialed Bobby's number again.

"What's that?"

"Bobby's phone went straight to voicemail." Once again it went to voicemail. He tried to call Bobby at his house, and Bobby's wife Pam answered the phone.

"Hello," she answered.

"Hey, Pam, it's Mike. How you doin'?"

"I'll do," Pam said, but Black could tell that something was wrong with her.

"Is Bobby there?"

"No that bastard ain't here."

"What's wrong, Pam?"

"I'm just tired of his shit, Mike."

"What happened, Pam?"

"I'm just sick and tired of his bitches callin' the house. I can't go through this again, Mike," Pam said.

"I understand, Pam. And you shouldn't have to. But Bobby told me it was just a misunderstanding. He didn't even know that woman like that," Black said, trying to be a friend and comfort her.

He liked Pam, felt like he owed her. Not only was Pam very helpful with Michelle before she went to live with his mother in Freeport, but it was Pam that saved Shy's life when Melinda tried to kill her.

"That's the same bullshit he told me," Pam said calmly. "And if that's the case, why does this bitch keep calling here?"

"She called again?"

"Called here again tonight."

"She did?" Black asked, surprised because he knew that Bobby had warned Ivillisa Ortiz not to call his house again.

"Yes, Mike, she did."

"What she want this time?"

"She called and asked to speak to Bobby. When I told her to stop calling here, she said to tell Bobby that Ivillisa Ortiz called and that a man named Lex was on his way there to kill her. When Bobby got home we argued about it and Bobby left. I can't go through this again, Mike."

"I know, Pam. Did Bobby say where he was going?"

"I guess he went to her."

"Okay, Pam. If Bobby calls, tell him I'm with Victor, and he can call me on his phone."

"I'll tell him," Pam said in a voice that Black hadn't heard since the night she killed Cat and Melinda. He ended the call and thought back to that night.

Black had been out dancing with Shy and they called Bobby to take them home, when Bobby got a call from Pam.

"I'm at your little girlfriend's apartment. I need you and Mike to come here now," Pam said and calmly hung up the phone.

When they arrived at the apartment it was in darkness, lit only by the streetlights shining through the window. When Bobby saw the gun in Pam's hand, Black stepped in front of him and Shy looked at him like he was crazy.

"What's up with the gun, Pam?" Black asked.

"It's for killing, Mike. You know better than most people what a gun is for," Pam said, obviously in a state of shock.

"Why don't you give me the gun, Pam?" Black asked quietly.

"Here," Pam said and handed the gun to Black. "I'm finished with it."

Now that she was no longer armed, Bobby stepped toward his wife again. "Pam," he said softly. "Where's Cat?"

"She's in the bedroom."

Bobby and Black went to the bedroom and opened the door. There on the floor was Cat with a gunshot wound in the chest. Pam very calmly explained that Cat had called the house again and said that she had just gotten finished fucking Bobby. After a round of bitch this and ho that, Cat said that she was going to take Bobby from Pam, and that she had broken into their house and was looking forward to fuckin' Bobby on their bed.

"That's when I hung up on her. But then I thought about it. This woman is crazy. So I called her back. I told her that we needed to talk face-to-face. I was surprised when she invited me over. We had small talk at the door when I first got here, and then she asked me to follow her. Said she wanted to show me something and led me straight to the bedroom. She opened the door and pointed to the bed. She said this is where she and Bobby fuck every day. That's when I shot her."

They took Pam to Black's house and left her with Shy while Black and Bobby disposed of the body. When they drove off, they drove right past Melinda, who had been following them all night. Melinda wanted to get back at Black for dumping her for Shy. She hated Shy with a passion and Melinda decided that whether she got Black back or not, that bitch Shy didn't deserve to live—even if it meant killing Black too.

With Pam resting comfortably, Shy went back downstairs and turned on the television. She had been channel surfing for awhile when Melinda stepped into the light, her gun was pointed at Shy. "How did you get in here?"

"I used to live here until you came along, bitch," Melinda said and took another step closer to Shy.

"What do you want?"

"I'm here to take back what you took from me."

"What are you talkin' about?"

"I'm talkin' about Black, you stupid bitch."

"And you think—"

"Shut up, bitch," Melinda said calmly. "You ruined everything. I was happy, we were happy; happy with each other, bitch. Do you understand what that means? Do you understand how I feel?"

Shy remained quiet.

"No, I didn't think so. You couldn't possibly under-stand what this feels like."

"You know you don't have to do this," Shy pleaded with Melinda.

"Oh, yes, I do. You don't deserve to have him. You don't deserve to have my man."

"We can talk about this, can't we?"

"Talk? Talk about what? How you snuck behind my back and stole my man? Is that what we should talk about, bitch? I don't think so. What do you think; if you keep me here talking that Black will come and save your worthless bitch-ass? Well, you can forget about that. I saw the body him and Bobby carried out. What, your girl Pam kill somebody?"

Shy didn't answer.

"It doesn't matter. You don't have to answer me, bitch. I know they took that body to the funeral parlor, and if they did, it'll be at least two hours before they get finished, so nobody is coming to save you."

If that was the case, Shy figured since she was going to die, she might as well speak her mind and die with dignity.

"You know what," Shy paused. "Damn, I don't even remember what your name is. Never was all that im-portant. But I guess it doesn't matter now. I guess noth-ing matters now. So let me tell you something. Mike Black is my man, bitch, not your man—my man." Shy held up her left hand. "This big-ass fuckin' rock on my finger proves that he's my man. He may have been your man, but you weren't woman enough to hold him, and that's why he's my man. So go ahead and kill me you

159

dumb bitch, 'cause even if you kill me, Mike Black will always be my man!"

Melinda grabbed the gun with both hands and cocked the hammer. Shy heard the shot, closed her eyes, and prepared to die.

But nothing happened.

Shy opened her eyes in time to see Melinda drop the gun and fall to the floor.

Pam stepped out of the shadows with a gun in her hand and stood over Melinda's body. "These bitches got to learn to stop fuckin' with somebody else's man."

Pam had killed two women that night and as a result, the stress of that traumatic experience caused her to suffer a nervous breakdown. Over the last couple of years her health had improved, but Black feared that this latest event might push Pam over the edge once again.

"We gotta find Bobby," Black told Victor. He knew that Bobby loved his wife and would do anything to avoid her having to go through what she had to endure because of his relationship with Cat. "He's on his way to this woman's apartment to make sure she stops calling Pam. Only problem is, I have no idea where she lives."

"I think I might know," Victor said as he drove.

"Where?"

"I can't be sure, but Sabrina said that she used to see Bobby's car outside a building on Grant Avenue."

Black laughed a little. "What was Sabrina doin' down there?"

"She was with Bo."

"Even better question: What was Bo doin' down there?" Black asked. Then he looked at Victor. "I know this is none of my business, and far be it for me to tell you who to lay the pipe to, but all I'm sayin' is be careful about fuckin' around with Sabrina. Niggas do stupid shit over a man fuckin' with his woman."

"I understand, Black," Victor said.

"You see how this shit is workin' out for Bobby."

Black was absolutely right about Bobby. As soon as Bobby heard about Ivillisa calling Pam, he left and headed straight for her apartment.

When Bobby got there, he could hear Ivillisa screaming as he came down the hall.

"I won't do it no more, I swear, Lex, please!"

Bobby banged on the door.

"Help me, please!" He heard Ivillisa yell.

Bobby took out his gun, kicked in the door and went inside the apartment. "Ivy!" he shouted.

"In the bedroom," Ivillisa yelled and tried to run away from Lex.

"Shut up!" Lex said and grabbed her by her hair. He began punching her in the face. When he let go of her hair, Ivillisa fell to the ground. Lex began kicking her just as Bobby appeared at the door. He looked at Ivillisa. Her once beautiful face was now a bloody mess. Her eye was swollen almost to the point of being shut. Her lip was busted and her clothes were torn.

Bobby ran up behind Lex and pulled him off her. Lex turned around and hit Bobby. Ivillisa got up and ran out of the room.

Lex grabbed Bobby's arm and the two men struggled for the gun. Lex forced Bobby's back against the wall and began banging his hand until Bobby dropped the gun. Lex hit Bobby in the face and then in the stomach.

161

"You think you can beat me old man?" he yelled as he grabbed Bobby and threw him to the floor.

Bobby got to his feet and rushed Lex, and the two men fell to the ground. They wrestled around until Bobby got on top and hit Lex several times in the face. Lex pushed Bobby off him, and got to his feet.

He picked up a lamp and swung it at Bobby, but he missed and Bobby rushed Lex again. The two traded blows until Bobby went down again. Lex stood over Bobby and kicked him. "Come on, get up!" Lex yelled.

Bobby caught Lex's foot as he tried to kick him, and jerked it. He went down near Bobby's gun and grabbed it. Lex stood up and pointed the gun at Bobby.

He looked at the barrel of the gun and knew he was about to die. At that moment, he thought about what he was about to die for.

Bobby thought about his wife and his children, and knew that whatever he was doing with Ivillisa Ortiz wasn't worth losing his family over, and it definitely wasn't worth dying for. Bobby heard the gunshot but felt no pain. He looked into Lex's eyes and watched him fall to the floor.

There stood Ivillisa, gun shaking in her hand. Bobby got up and took the gun from Ivillisa. "Took you long enough."

"I had to find where he put his gun," Ivillisa said.

Bobby looked at Lex and pried his gun from Lex's dead hand. "I'm gettin' too old for this shit."

Ivillisa threw her arms around Bobby. He kissed her on the forehead and removed her arms from around his neck.

"Come on," Bobby said and took Ivillisa by the hand and led her out of the apartment.

"What about him?" Ivillisa said as she looked down at Lex's body.

"Don't worry about him. I'll call somebody to take care of him. Right now, you need to get out of here."

"Where are we going?" she asked.

"A friend of mine is a doctor. He'll fix you up and make sure you're all right."

It wasn't too long after Bobby and Ivillisa left that Black and Victor got to her building. They didn't see his car but they went inside anyway.

Victor approached a man in the lobby. He told them which apartment she lived in. When they got to the door and found it cracked open, they went in with guns drawn. They looked around the apartment until Victor found Lex's body. "In here, Black."

Black went to the door and looked in. "See what I'm sayin'. That could be you dead over fuckin' around with Sabrina."

"True that, but I prefer to look at it as that being Bo," Victor said and followed Black out of the apartment.

CHAPTER TWENTY-ONE

Kirk finally got a break in his case. Earlier in the day, he got a call from Reyes, the head of the CSI team who told Kirk that they found some evidence at one of the murder scenes. Kirk and Richards went back to the precinct to see what he had.

"What you got, Reyes?" Kirk said as soon as he came through the door.

"How are you, detective?" Reyes said.

"Fine."

"I was talking to Richards," Reyes said and laughed.

"You gotta forgive my partner," Richards said and shook hands with Reyes as Kirk took a seat. "He gets so caught up in these things that he sometimes forgets his manners."

"Fuck this, what you got, Reyes," Kirk said.

Reyes handed Kirk a file. "My team found a fingerprint at one of your crime scenes that didn't match any of your bodies."

"One of the shooter's maybe?" Richards speculated.

"We should be that lucky," Kirk said as he opened the file.

"The prints belong to a woman. Her name is Erika Thompson," Reyes told them.

"Arrest record includes shoplifting, possession with the intent to distribute and solicitation," Kirk said as he read over the file.

"Doesn't sound like a shooter, but maybe she can tell us something," Richards said.

"Thanks, Reyes. We'll check it out," Kirk said, and he and Richards left the office.

Within a few hours, one of Kirk's informants told him where to find her on the street, working a corner.

"That's her," Richards said as the detectives sat in their car. "What's your plan? If we rollup on them in this car, they'll all scatter and we might lose her."

"Why don't you walk up to her, see if she makes you an offer?"

"Why me?"

"'Cause they'd never believe a good-looking guy like me would be out here tryin' to buy some pussy. But you, on the other hand," Kirk said and laughed. "You got trick written all over you."

"Fuck you, Kirk. That's all I gotta say; fuck you," Richards said and got out of the car.

Kirk let Richards get a little ways down the street before he got out of the car. He approached slowly and looked on as Richards walked up to the women on the corner and began talking to Erika Thompson.

"Oh, I got what you want, honey."

"Well let's go then."

"Hey, hey, slow down. You at least got a car or something?"

"Yeah, come on," Richards said and grabbed her hand.

"It's gonna cost you," Erika said as he practically dragged her along.

"How much?"

"Head is fifty. It's a hundred for the whole show."

"That much, huh?"

"You gotta pay for what you want. And I can tell you want this pussy *real* bad," she said when he got in the car.

"Yeah, and you're under arrest," Richards said and showed her his badge.

"Damn," Erika said and tried to get out of the car.

"Took you long enough." Kirk got in the back seat and grabbed her. "Where you goin', honey?"

"This is fucked up. This is fuckin' entrapment, that's what this is, entrapment."

"Whatever you say," Richards said as he put the cuffs on her.

When they got to the station and had a female officer search her, they found that she was carrying a small quantity of rock cocaine. After being processed, Erika was taken to an interrogation room where she was left alone for over an hour.

Finally, Kirk and Richards came into the room. They both sat down and began to read Erika's arrest record to her.

Erika sat quietly and listened. "Okay, so what y'all really want?"

"What do you mean?" Richards asked.

"Like you been tellin' me, this ain't my first time at this. I'm in here 'cause y'all want something."

"Okay," Kirk said and stood up. He handed Richards an envelope and Richards laid the pictures out in front of Erika. The look in her eyes told them that she recognized the men in the pictures. "Those three men were murdered last night. Your fingerprints were found at the scene."

"What?" Erika looked at the two detectives. "You think I did that shit?"

"Didn't you?" Richards asked. "Like you said, we don't have you sittin' in here for just some solicitation beef. You killed those men and stole their coke, didn't you?"

"Oh hell no! I didn't do that shit. I swear 'for God, I didn't kill nobody."

Richards looked at Kirk and laughed. "When was the last time we heard that one?"

"Last time we questioned a murder suspect."

"I didn't kill nobody!" Erika yelled.

"Then how did your prints get there?"

"Okay, okay, look, I was there, but I didn't kill them niggas."

Richards slid a notepad in front of Erika. "Just go ahead and write down how you killed them and it will go a lot easier for you."

"Oh hell no," Erika said and pushed the pad back at Richards. "I ain't writing shit 'cause I ain't kill them niggas."

Kirk got in her face. "Then tell us who did."

"If I tell you what I know, what I get outta it?"

"She wants to deal," Richards said. "I think we should just go ahead and book her for murder.

"What is you sayin'? This shit is crazy. I'm tellin' you I didn't kill nobody."

Kirk shrugged his shoulders and started to leave the room. Richards got up and followed him to the door. "Wait a minute, wait a minute, damn. I'll tell you what I know."

Kirk came back to the table and sat down. "I'm listening."

"I was there in the apartment when the shit went down, but I'm tellin' you, it wasn't me that did the shootin'."

"What happened?"

"I was there to get a hit and they let me use the bathroom to smoke. So I'm in there smokin' when all of a sudden I hear the shootin'."

"What did you do?"

"I dove in the bathtub and stayed there for a while after the shooting stopped. When I came out everybody was dead."

"What did you do then?"

"I searched the place."

"What'd you find?" Richards asked.

"I found the rock you caught me with, and I got out of there."

"You know who supplied these guys?"

"Nope. All I can tell you is that it's a woman."

"A woman?" Richards questioned.

"I don't know who she is, but they was always talkin' about her."

"Well tell me this one more thing, and I'll see what I can do on the solicitation and possession charges."

"What else y'all wanna know?"

"Who would you buy from now that your friends here are dead?"

"Rockwell."

"Who?"

"KK Rockwell. I can tell you where to find him."

CHAPTER TWENTY-TWO

After drinking at Cynt's with Bobby, the phone ringing was the last thing Nick wanted to hear. He reached in his pocket and pulled out the phone. "What!"

"Damn, nigga, why you gotta answer the phone like that?" Rain said.

"What do you want, Rain?"

"What the fuck's wrong with you?"

"Nothing. What do you want, Rain?"

"We got shit that needs doin'."

"What I don't need is your ass tryin' to tell me what the fuck I gotta do," Nick yelled and hung up the phone.

He held the phone in his hand because he knew it wouldn't take Rain long to call back. When the phone rang again he answered it. "What do you want?"

"I told you. We got shit to do today and you fuckin' around."

"What?"

"What you mean what?"

"What we gotta do?"

"Shit, mutha fucka, you already know what we gotta do."

"It waited this long, another couple of hours ain't gonna make no difference. I'll get wit' you later."

"Wait!" Rain yelled.

"What?"

"Nick, listen to me for a second. I got some important shit goin' on over here right now. I need your help with it. You the only one that can handle this," Rain pleaded.

"When shit was goin' your way you didn't need my help, now I'm the only one who can handle it?"

"Yes. Now come on. Get over here as fast as you can. It's real fuckin' important."

"What's goin' on over there?"

"I don't wanna say over the phone. It's just that deep. But I'm for real 'bout this. You need to come handle this shit for real."

"All right. I'll be there."

"How long you gonna be?"

"I'll be there when I fuckin' get there!"

"All right, nigga. You ain't gotta yell and shit. Just hurry your ass up. This shit is important," Rain said and Nick hung up the phone.

When he got to Rain's apartment she was naked when she answered the door. He walked past her like Rain being naked was no big deal.

"What was so important?"

"What is your problem? Why you givin' me all this fuckin' attitude?"

Nick grabbed Rain by the arm and pulled her to him. "I asked you what was so fuckin' important that you needed me to deal with right away?"

Rain jerked her arm away from him. "You don't see nothin' important here?"

Nick looked around. "All I see is you."

"Shit. That's what's important."

"What?"

"I ain't seen your ass all day. I need some of that dick."

"That's all you wanted? To fuck?"

"Hell yeah, I told you, this pussy is deep and only you can handle it," Rain said and laughed a little.

"You want me to fuck you?" Nick grabbed Rain by the throat. "You want to get fucked? All right," he said and began unbuckling his pants. "You wanna get fucked!" Nick spun Rain around quickly and bent her over the couch. He pushed himself inside her and started trying to tear that pussy up.

"What's wrong with you today?" Rain wanted to know as he pounded away.

Nick grabbed a handful of her hair and pulled her head back. "You want me to stop?"

"Oh, hell no. Go on and get this pussy. It's been throbbin' for you all day."

Nick reached out and grabbed Rain by the shoulder with one hand and her waist with the other. He bent his knees and pulled her to him as hard as she could stand it. "That's it, nigga. Get this pussy."

He felt himself start to swell inside her, so Nick pulled out. He grabbed Rain by the hand and pulled her to the dining room table. Rain hopped up on it and lifted her legs. Nick grabbed her ankles and slammed himself into her.

He hammered away while Rain alternated between squeezing her nipples and playing with clit. After awhile he pulled her up and Rain wrapped her legs around his waist, and her arms around his neck.

They got into a slow grind, almost like they were dancing. Nick felt her body trembling and Rain raked her nails across his back. "You gonna make me cum!" Rain shouted. He pulled out of her when he felt her juices dripping down his legs.

Rain hopped down from the table, bent over and took Nick into her mouth. He stood as still as he could for a while, enjoying the sight of his dick disappearing and reappearing as it went deeper and deeper in and out of her mouth. Rain moaned and fingered herself while she sucked his dick.

"Come on." This time it was Rain that grabbed Nick by the hand and pulled him to the couch. Rain pushed him down. Then she turned around and straddled his legs. With her left hand she spread her cheek, reached for his dick with the other and guided Nick inside her.

Rain leaned forward, put her hands on his knees, and began to bounce up and down on it. She had a big round ass, so Nick laid back and enjoyed the view. He spanked that ass with both hands and then began to slam it down on his lap. Rain ran her fingers through her hair and pumped harder.

Then she stopped suddenly, turned around and got right back on and rode Nick until she came again.

"You got a bitch cummin' all over your dick!" Rain rolled off of him and sat down on the couch.

After she caught her breath, she got up and started looking around for her cigarettes. Nick had other ideas.

"I ain't nowhere near finished fuckin' you."

Nick got up and snatched the cigarettes out of her hand and dragged her into the bedroom. He pushed her down on the bed. Rain moved around on the bed and he entered her again.

Since he was in no rush at all to cum, Nick got up on his hands and long dicked her for a long while, sliding in and out of her slowly. Pulling himself almost completely out of her and then back inside slowly, as deep as he could get it. "That's right, nigga, get all your pussy."

Rain came again, but Nick still wasn't done with her. He lay down between her legs and lifted them as high as he could, then eased two fingers of one hand inside her, and gently massaged her clit until Rain began to squirm. He peeled back the foreskin around her clit and flicked the tip of his tongue across it. Nick ran his tongue up and down her moist lips and then back to her clit.

Every now and then he would look up and watch her squeezing her nipples. Rain had juicy titties and fat nipples. She held his head in place and pressed her hips in his face. Rain began rocking her hips and before long, she came again.

But Nick still wasn't done with her.

Once again he spread her legs and entered her. Nick was ready to explode inside her and thrust himself hard and deep inside her. Rain held onto him tight and matched his movements. By now, her pussy was dripping wet, just the way he liked it. Nick began to move faster and Rain picked up her pace to match his. He could tell from the look on her face that she could feel him expanding inside her.

"That's it, nigga, cum hard in your pussy!"

Nick's eyes opened wide, his body became rigid, and he began rocking his hips. Nick held onto it for as long as he could, and only let it go when he couldn't stand it any longer. Nick rolled off of her and lay flat on his back.

CHAPTER TWENTY-THREE

Rain opened her eyes and got in a good stretch before she rolled out of bed. Her body felt so good; she really *needed* to be loved like that. She looked over at Nick. He was out for the count. There was a part of her that wanted to let him sleep, but there was work that needed to be put in.

"Wake up," Rain said as he shook Nick.

"What?"

"Come on, get up. We got shit to do."

When Nick rolled over and opened his eyes. Rain was dressed and ready to go. "What's your rush?"

"We need to find the mutha fuckas that's robbin' me and we ain't gonna find 'em layin' up in bed."

"That was your idea."

"So I wanted some dick; something wrong with that?"

"Not at all."

"All right then, we done fuckin'. Now it's time to get to work."

"Where we goin'?" Nick asked. He propped two pillows behind his head and made himself comfortable.

"I don't know yet. But like I said, we ain't gonna find 'em layin' around here."

176

"I know that, but we been out there lookin' for them and what have we accomplished? You killed some niggas that didn't get us no closer to findin' what we lookin' for."

Rain sat down on the edge of the bed. "So what you think we should do?" she asked.

"Wait for them to come to us," Nick answered.

"What you talkin' 'bout? You think they gonna show up here?"

"No, but they might. But what I'm sayin' is we know that the mutha fuckas been robbin' your spots, right?"

"Right."

"All we gotta do is figure out where they gonna hit next and be there waitin' for them."

"I never thought of that."

"Yeah I know," Nick said matter-of-factly. "So who do you think they gonna hit next?"

"I ain't got but two more spots."

"So pick one. Which one is the bigger target?"

"Rockwell."

Once he was showered and dressed, Nick and Rain left the apartment and headed for the Taurus. On the way, Nick put on his gloves. Other than telling her that it was over between him and Wanda, he didn't have much to say while Rain drove to the spot. He was still bothered by losing Wanda over this mess and what would happen when the story got back to Black. It didn't matter how caught up in their legit businesses he was, sooner or later it would get back to him.

Once the truth became known, there would be questions about how it had effected their arrangement with Angelo and Stark. Then there was Wanda. She would definitely mention it to Black. And the result of that would be more questions.

When they got to the spot that was run by Rockwell, everybody was on edge. They had heard what had happened at her other spots and they all wondered if they were next. Nick and Rain talked to them for a while, neither mentioning that they had come there expecting that this would be the bandits' next target. After awhile, as business proceeded the way it normally did, Nick and Rain went in the back room and waited.

They had been there for over an hour and were starting to think that they were wrong, and then it began. "Everybody down!"

When Rain heard that, she pulled her gun and went for the door. "Wait!" Nick tried to stop her. He wanted to wait until they had everybody tied up before they made their move. Before he could get to her, Rain was out the door. "Damn!" Nick said and went after her.

The second they saw Rain come out the room they opened up on her right then. Nick made it out of there in time to see three masked men. One of them had shot Rain's people who were on their knees; another was firing at Rain while the other was trying to gather up the drugs from the kitchen. He fired at Nick. Nick took aim and returned fire. He hit him with three shots: one in the shoulder, one in his hand and one in the leg, before ducking back in the room. There was two more standing by the door firing shots in his direction. He looked around for Rain; she had taken cover behind the couch and was trying to reload her weapon.

When they stopped firing, Nick came out of the room. With a gun in each hand, Nick hit one with two shots in his chest; the other started to run out of the apartment. Rain got up and went after him. Nick shot him before he made it out the door.

Rain walked up to him and kicked the gun away from him. She then pulled the mask off him. "You know him?" Nick asked as he unmasked the other.

"Never seen him before," Rain said and shot him in the head.

Nick went in the kitchen to the only survivor. When he got there, Nick heard another gun go off. He turned quickly and pointed his weapon. Rain was standing over the other man. She shot him in the head, too. Nick lowered his weapon and grabbed the man in the kitchen. He pulled him to his feet and pulled off his mask. Rain was about to shoot him but Nick stopped her. "Don't you wanna know who sent them?"

Nick put the barrel of his gun in the bullet wound in his shoulder and pressed down on it. "Who sent you?"

He screamed in pain, but didn't say anything. Nick took his other gun and shot the man in the knee. He screamed again. "Jay! Jay Easy sent us," the man said through gritted teeth.

Rain put her gun to the man's head. "Jay Easy sent you?" she asked.

"Who's Jay Easy?" Nick asked.

"A dead mutha fucka," Rain said and pulled the trigger. She looked around the apartment until she found a duffel bag. Rain gathered up all of her product and walked out of the apartment.

Once they had driven away from the building, Nick turned to Rain. "So who's Jay Easy?"

"Nigga used to be my dog. Remember? I told you about him; got cracked over some stupid shit. Me and him just got through takin' care of a problem, and I gave him the guns and told him to get rid of them 'cause they was both hot. But before he got to do it, he decides he needs to stop and get some cigarettes. When he leaves the store he gets pulled over. Cops search the car, find the guns. Guns got bodies on them. Jay Easy goes down for murder. But he got out on a technicality. His lawyer said the search was an illegal search."

"Why?"

"Said cops didn't have no reason to stop him, so they ain't have no reason to search the car."

"You seen him since he been out?"

"Yeah, he came by the club one night. I told him we was done, you know, 'cause I was fuckin' wit' you and shit."

"You know where to find him?"

"Yeah, that's where we goin' now. He hangs out at a little bar up on the avenue."

When they got to the spot, Nick started to get out of the car, but Rain stopped him. "What?"

"Let me go in alone and bring him out."

"This mutha fucka is tryin' to take you down and you wanna go in by yourself?"

Rain smiled at Nick. "If I walked up to you and offered you some of this pussy, wouldn't you come with me?" she said and got out of the car.

Since he couldn't argue with her logic, Nick got out of the front and got in the back seat. Ten minutes later, Rain came out of the bar with Jay Easy on her arm. Nick ducked down and waited for them to get in the car.

As soon as Rain was in the car, Jay Easy tried to kiss her. Nick put a gun to his head. "Slow down, playa."

"Shit!" Jay Easy said and put up his hands.

Rain reached over and took his gun. She put the gun on her lap.

"You always was a sneaky bitch, Rain," Jay Easy said.

Rain punched him in the face. "I got your sneaky bitch," she said and punched him again. Rain started up the car and drove away. "I rolled up on your shooters tonight. They're dead."

"I don't know what the fuck you're talkin' 'bout. What shooters?"

Rain punched him in the face again. "Don't lie to me, nigga! One of your boys told us you sent 'em before I blew his brains out. Be a fuckin' man and admit that shit before I kill your bitch-ass."

Jay Easy looked over his shoulder at Nick. "I thought we had something. I was ready to do life for you. I gets out and come lookin' for my woman and you play me off for this nigga."

"So you decide to start robbin' me?"

"I still got all the dope and the money. After I shut you down I was gonna step to you and give it all back."

"Bullshit! After all this shit you was just gonna hand it all back to me."

"Yeah. I wanted to show you that you needed me in your life. Not this nigga! He can't do the shit for you that I can. He couldn't stop a nigga like me."

Nick pressed the gun to his temple. "See how well that worked out for you so far, playboy," he said.

"Go ahead and do it. But even if you kill me the shit won't stop. It will only get worse. You got more enemies than just me. Only one that can save you is me. Drop this nigga and make it all right, and we can get back to where we was," Jay Easy pleaded.

Rain looked at Jay Easy and shook her head. "You always was a stupid mutha fucka. I don't want you. That nigga's so far above your level that you couldn't even understand it." Rain laughed. "That, and he's fuckin' the shit outta me."

Jay Easy spit in her face. Rain picked up the gun and shot him in the face. Then she pulled the car over and pushed him out in the street. Rain closed the door and drove off.

CHAPTER TWENTY-FOUR

One step behind, Kirk and Richards arrive at Rockwell's apartment. When they get there, the uniformed officers had already gotten there and had taken control of the murder scene.

"Looks like we're a little late for the party," Richards said as he and Kirk entered the apartment.

Kirk looked around the apartment. "Yeah, but this one's different." He knelt down next to one of Rain's people. "They're not tied up this time." He stood up and walked around the room. "Looks like somebody got them before they had a chance to tie them up, and killed the shooters."

"PR?"

"Probably," Kirk said and continued walking around the apartment. He looked at the bullet holes in the wall. "Looks like she was in the back here; they see her and start shooting at her."

"You're not sayin' that she took all three of these guys down by herself, are you?" Richards asked.

"I doubt it, but I'm not ruling it out. We'll know more when the ballistics comes back. That may tell us how many, and if we're lucky, who was with her."

Kirk went in the kitchen and looked at the body. "Come here, Pat." When Richards got there, Kirk pointed to the wounds. "This one was shot once in the shoulder, once in his hand, once in each leg and the kill shot to the head; like they were trying to make him talk."

"Think he told them what they wanted to know?"

"If he did we can expect more bodies," Kirk said. "Anybody see anything?" he said to one of the uniforms.

"Haven't started a canvass yet, detective."

"Well get to it. Maybe a miracle will occur and somebody saw something."

While the officers went to canvass the building, the detectives remained at the crime scene. "What do we have, Pat?"

"So far we got four crime scenes. The first three were most likely drug robberies. The victims were all tied up, on their knees and executed. Word is, all the victims work for somebody called PR—who a junkie hooker says is a woman. She tips us to this place.

"We get here and we find six bodies. One of them is probably Rockwell. Three of them were most likely the shooters we've been looking for, and one of them may have been tortured into telling PR or somebody connected to her, *who knows what* before they blow his brains out," Kirk said and walked back in the kitchen. "Too bad he can't tell us what he told them. At least we'd know where to go next."

"You guys throw a party and didn't invite me?"

Kirk and Richards turned to see Detective Sanchez walk in the apartment. "What? You didn't get the memo about killing drug dealers?" Richards mused.

"I must have missed that one. Que Pasa, Kirk?"

"Gene."

"I take it these are the shooters you been looking for? I'd ask if you killed them," Sanchez said as he looked at one of the bodies, "but shooting suspects in the head isn't exactly your style."

"You recognize anybody?" Kirk asked.

Sanchez walked around the room and checked each of the bodies. "This one."

"Who is he?" Richards asked.

"KK Rockwell."

"You know who he's with?" Richards asked.

"He used to run with a chick named Rain Robinson."

"Who's she?" Kirk asked.

"You remember Jasper Robinson?"

"Yeah—used to run few gambling spots back in the day."

"Rain is his daughter. She was a small timer; a little coke, a little heroin when she could get it. But my sources tell me that she retired and took over JR's night club and his gambling interests after her father died."

"PR?" Richards asked.

"Could be," Kirk said as one of the uniformed officers came in the room.

"Detectives, I just talked to a lady who saw a man and a woman leaving the building after she heard the shots; said they got in a gray Taurus."

"She give you a license number?"

"No sir."

"What about a description?"

"She didn't get a good look at them. Only that they looked like they were in a hurry."

"Thank you, officer. Go ahead and get that out on the wire."

"Already done, detective, and we got a report that a gray Taurus was seen in the area of another murder."

"Another one?" Sanchez asked.

Kirk looked in the kitchen at the dead man. "I guess you gave somebody up. Any details?"

"Witness said the Taurus stopped, pushed the body out and drove away."

"Think we should take a look?" Richards asked.

"No, I'd rather ride by JR's and see what Miss Robinson has to say about all this," Kirk said, and him and Richards left the apartment and headed for JR's.

CHAPTER TWENTY-FIVE

Nick and Rain were on the way back to her apartment when her cell phone rang. "This Rain."

"You need to get down to the club," a female voice said.

"Who is this?"

"It's Rose from the club."

"What's goin' on?"

"We got robbed."

"What?"

"I said—"

"I heard you. What happened?"

"Five of them came through the back door with guns. Two of them hit the safe in the office and the other three took the gambling room."

"Goddamn it!" Rain shouted. "These niggas gonna break my ass. Did anybody get hurt?"

"Not bad, but somebody called the cops. They're all over the place."

"Did they find the gambling room?"

"Not yet, but—"

"I'll be down there," Rain said and ended the call. She looked at Nick. "Somebody hit the club. Rose says cops is all over the place. But they haven't found the gambling spot."

"You know how much they got?" Nick asked.

"I don't know. I won't know until we get there," Rain said and drove a little faster.

When Rain slowed down for a red light, Nick turned to her and said, "Let me out here."

"What? Didn't you hear what I said? Somebody robbed the club and the gambling spot."

"Yeah, I heard you. Did you hear me? Let me out here," Nick said again.

Rain stopped short and Nick reached for the handle. "What is wrong with you?"

"Nothing's wrong. I just got something I need to do right now."

"What you got to do that's more important than this?"

"Right now, what I'm gonna do is more important. So you go deal with what you gotta deal with and I'll get with you later."

"Are you serious? I need you with me on this."

"For what? Whatever happened is already over and done with. What you need me for?"

Rain had no answer.

"I didn't think so. You go on, handle your business. I'll get with you later and we'll talk about who your enemies are, and how many more there are."

"You not runnin' out on me, are you?"

"No, Rain, I'm not runnin' out on you. I got too much invested in you for that to happen," Nick said and thought about Wanda.

He got out of the car and watched as Rain drove away fast. He walked down to next corner and hailed a cab. "Where to?"

"Just drive," Nick said and thought about what he was gonna do next. He took out his cell phone and started to call Monika. Before it started to ring, he ended the call and put the phone away. He knew that he was gonna need backup, but Monika wasn't the one he needed on this one.

At this point, Monika was too tied to Black. She had become Black's personal assassin. He wasn't willing to put her in a position where she would have to keep something from him, much less have to lie to him. This was his cross to bear.

Nick took the phone out again and held it in his hand for awhile. Then he dialed Bobby's number. It went straight to voicemail. Then he tried calling him at the club. "Impressions, this is Tara."

"Tara, its Nick."

"What's up, Nick?"

"Is Bobby there?"

"I'm not sure. Hold on, let me check," Tara said and put Nick on hold.

He had been on hold for about five minutes and was about to hang up when Bobby came to the phone. "Hello."

"Bobby, its Nick."

"What's up, Nick?"

"I need you to do something with me."

"What you need?"

"I'll tell about it when I see you. You remember that thing we talked about earlier?"

"Yeah," Bobby said and immediately had a good idea what Nick had in mind.

"Meet me outside."

"I'm on my way," Bobby told Nick.

"How long before you get there?"

"Give me thirty minutes."

"See you there."

Nick told the driver where to go and leaned back. He thought about his history with Bobby. Things have gotten better between him and Bobby, but Nick knew that he'd never forget that night. It should have never happened; but Nick was gone, too far gone. Her name was Camille Augustus.

Nick knew when he met her that she was with Bobby, but it didn't matter. He had to have her. Nick had never met any woman like Camille. She was fascinating to be around and to talk to. The way she talked with that thick Barbados accent. And she was beautiful; her dark complexion, her flawless body, and those dark eyes.

Thoughts of that night used to haunt Nick like a bad dream that would never end. Bobby with his gun in Nick's mouth, screaming that he was gonna kill both Nick and Camille. Black with his gun to Bobby's head—"Bobby, please," he pleaded quietly. "Take the gun out of his mouth and put it down."

Nick and Bobby had made peace and put that all behind them. Now Bobby was the only one that Nick could depend on. *Funny how things come around,* Nick thought as the cab got to Fat Larry's. He saw Bobby's CLK350 Cabriolet car parked outside. "Pull over by that Benz," Nick told the cab driver.

He got in the car with Bobby and told him what had happened with Rain. "How you wanna play it?" Bobby asked.

"I just wanna talk," Nick answered.

"Your show," Bobby said and put on his gloves. Nick already had his on. They got out and went to the door. The restaurant was closed but Nick saw Stark's car parked in the alley. They banged on the door and Moon came and let them in.

"What's up, Bobby. What's up, Nick," he said.

"Where's Stark?" Bobby asked.

"He's in the back. Come on," Moon said and they followed him to the back of the restaurant. When they got in to office, Stark got up and came from behind his desk.

"Bobby, Nick, what brings y'all down here?" Stark said and they shook hands.

"I need to talk to you about something," Nick said.

"What's up?" Stark asked. Bobby looked at Moon. "Would you excuse us for a minute, Moon?"

"No problem," Moon said and left the office.

When Moon closed the door, Stark sat down on the edge of his desk. Nick stepped to him.

"You selling product to Rain?"

Stark looked at Nick and Bobby. "She tell you that?"

"No, she didn't give you up. It was just something she said or didn't say that made me think that you were."

Stark dropped his head and laughed a little. "Yeah, I—" but before he could finish his sentence, Bobby was on him.

He grabbed Stark by the throat and shoved his gun in Stark's mouth. "Do you realize the position that puts

Black in? The position it puts all of us in?" Bobby said softly.

Stark nodded his head.

"You heard about what's going on with Rain?" Nick asked.

Stark nodded his head.

"Kirk been to see you, hasn't he?" Nick asked.

Stark nodded his head.

"You know it's not gonna take long for him to connect you to Rain, and you to us," Nick said calmly.

Stark nodded his head.

"You knew this shit could happen, but you did it anyway. But she was runnin' a good program for a while. Quiet. And she was bringing you plenty of money. If this shit wasn't happening and she didn't have to tell me about it, it would still be all good."

Bobby's grip got a little tighter. "So you been sittin' in Black's face all this time, and all the while you got your knife in his back," Bobby said.

Stark nodded his head.

"If you live long enough, you'll learn that loyalty is worth more than money," Nick said and Bobby eased the gun out of Stark's mouth.

Stark reached for his throat and tried to catch his breath. "Black know about Rain?" he asked.

"Not yet," Bobby said. "And for your sake you better hope he doesn't find out." He turned his back to Stark and put a silencer on his gun.

"Rain is done as far as you're concerned, understand?" Nick told him.

"Yeah, I understand," Stark said still gasping for air. "What can I do to make this right?" he asked.

192

"I just told you. It ends tonight," Nick said and Bobby followed him to the door.

When Bobby got to the door he turned around and raised his weapon. Both Stark and Nick looked at Bobby as he pointed the weapon at Stark.

"What's up, Bobby?" Stark asked.

"Like Nick said, for you, it ends tonight," Bobby said and put three in Stark's chest.

Nick looked at Stark's body on the floor and then at Bobby. "What happened to *it's your show*?"

"This nigga betrayed all of us. He had to die. Now, question is, what you gonna do with Moon?" Bobby asked.

Nick shook his head and opened the office door. He saw Moon sitting at a table near the office. "Moon, could you come here for a minute." Nick closed the door and put a silencer on his gun.

Moon got up and headed for the office. He opened the door and stepped in. He saw Stark's body on the floor. He was about to reach for his gun when Bobby closed the door and Nick put two bullets in the back of his head.

They left the office and locked the door. They exited Fat Larry's through the back door. Nick got in the car with Bobby and they drove off. "What you gonna do now?" Bobby asked.

"I know one thing. I gotta cut Rain loose," Nick said.

"It's too late for that now," Bobby said without looking at Nick. "It's gone way past you just cuttin' her loose."

Nick looked at Bobby and knew that he was right. "I'm gonna have to kill her," Nick said without emotion,

but the idea of having to kill Rain was tearing him up
inside.

CHAPTER TWENTY-SIX

Since they arrived at the apartment of Ivillisa Ortiz looking for Bobby and finding Lex dead, Black and Victor had been in the street. They had gone by Impressions and were told by Tara that Bobby was there, but he left after getting a call from Nick. But when Black told Tara to call Nick, she got no answer.

They were about to leave the club when Tara came rushing to the front door to stop them.

"Black! Wait a minute," Tara yelled.

"What's up?"

"You got a call in the office," she said, trying to catch her breath.

"Who is it?" Black asked as they returned to the office.

"It's Angelo Collette."

When Black got to the office and picked up the phone, Angelo, to his surprise, was still holding.

"What's up, Angee?"

"For Christ's sake, Mikey, you need to get a fuckin' phone. At least while Kevon was around somebody could get in touch with you, but now that he's dead, you know how many places I had to call to get you?"

"Sorry, Angee. You know I don't like being all that accessible."

"And believe me I understand why you feel that way. I mean, there are times when I wanna throw this fuckin' thing out the fuckin' window."

"Then why don't you? Not havin' one works just fine with me. One less place a mutha fucka can listen to you."

"You got a point."

"What you got for me?"

"You feel like ridin' out to Brooklyn?"

"Not really."

"Well, if you wanna talk to Oleg tonight you'll be at his uncle's restaurant in Brighton Beach at midnight."

"Good look."

"He'll be there waiting for you."

"Thanks, Angee. Save that bottle of Rémy for me. I'll get with you in a couple of days."

"You do that."

It was just after midnight when Black and Victor pulled up in front of a restaurant on Neptune Avenue in the Brighton Beach section of Brooklyn. The place was closed when they arrived. Victor knocked on the door.

"Yes," the large man said when he opened the door.

"Mike Black to see Oleg Mushnikov," Victor said.

The KGB targeted Oleg for recruitment even before he graduated. He spent seventeen years as a mid-level agent in the KGB's foreign intelligence wing, rising to the rank of lieutenant colonel. After a few years spying on foreigners in Leningrad, he attended the elite foreign intelligence training institute, and then was assigned to work with East Germany intelligence, the Stasi, and the raw intelligence was sent directly to Moscow.

The downfall of communism left an economic, moral and social vacuum. Oleg began to fill the gap, supplying luxury items, jeans, cigarettes, vodka, chewing gum and stereo equipment to those who could afford them. Then he got involved with members of Izmaylovskaya that were running prostitution and gambling rings in Sri Lanka and scheming with the Colombian drug cartel. Once they tried to sell their newfound Colombian friends a Soviet-era submarine.

The man stepped to one side and allowed them to enter. Black saw Oleg sitting alone at a table near the back of the restaurant. Oleg waved for him to come back. Black handed both of his guns to the man who opened the door and made his way to the table. Victor surrendered his weapon and took a seat at the bar.

Oleg stood up to greet him. "Mikhail," Oleg said, calling Black by the Russian name for Michael.

"How's it goin', Oleg?" Black said, and the two men shook hands. "I know that you are a busy man. Thank you for agreeing to see me."

"Please sit," Oleg urged. "You know, when Mr. Angelo Collette calls and says Mr. Mikhail Black wants to talk to me, I say, oh no, I have no Rémy Martin for him to drink." Oleg pointed at his man, and he brought a bottle of Rémy and placed it on the table in front of Black, along with two glasses. "I sent someone to find a bottle so we can drink together."

"Thank you, Oleg. This means a lot," Black said and reached for the bottle. He poured a drink for himself and Oleg.

Both men shot their drinks and Black poured another. "I tell you something else. When Mr. Angelo Collette calls and says to me Mr. Mikhail Black wants to talk to me, I say to myself, what is the reason for this? I have my suspicions about a reason, but still, I wonder. I have shared a bottle with you many times, but never has Mr. Mikhail Black wanted to talk. Drink yes, talk no. So, I am wondering, what it is that brings you to me?"

"Are you familiar with a woman named Jada West?"

"Yes," Oleg said slowly and curiously. "I am familiar with Jada West." Oleg picked up his glass and pointed at Black. "You surprise me my friend. This was not what I was thinking you wanted to talk about. Now tell me, what business is this of yours?"

"Ms. West tells me that you've shown an interest in her business."

Oleg sat back in his chair and smiled. "This woman, this madam, this Jada West, she belong to you?"

"No, Oleg, Ms. West is a personal friend. I have no interest in her business."

"Now I am wondering, why are you here?"

"I came to ask you as a favor to me, to forget about Ms. West and her business."

Oleg laughed when he heard that. Then he reached for the bottle and poured them both a drink. Oleg held up his glass and Black followed suit before both men shot their drinks. "You, me, Mr. Angelo Collette, we have done this many times before, but this is the first time you have ever asked me for anything other than to pass the bottle. I do not know whether I should be honored or insulted that you ask me this now."

"That was a mistake on my part. Please believe me, I meant you no insult. We should have had a conversation about business long before now."

"I wish that we had too. But your business is gambling. Mr. Angelo Collette, his business is extortion and narcotics. Me, I am just a poor Russian trying to earn a living in your wonderful country. Now you come to me and say Oleg, you cannot earn a living because Jada West is a friend."

Black put down his glass. "Oleg, listen to me. If you were willing to forget about Ms. West and her business, I think there are some things that you and I can work on that in the long run, would be much profitable for you and your associates, should you choose to involve them."

"What did you have in mind?" Oleg asked, seemingly intrigued by what Black was telling him. Oleg was always looking for ways to make money, which was how Jada West came to his attention.

"My partners and I are looking to make some investments in Russia," Black said. "In order to make that happen, we need a presence in Russia; a Russian presence. In exchange for your consideration about Ms. West, I would talk to my associates about taking you on as a partner."

"What type of businesses we talking about?"

Black thought back to the last meeting he had with Meka Brazil and tried to remember what she said about foreign investment in Russia. "There's a company that makes multimedia switching gear for cable companies that just got certification for its product line in Russia. Communications infrastructure investment could represent a significant opportunity," Black said, trying to repeat what Meka said, but Oleg didn't seem impressed. "Then there's wind."

"Wind?"

"Are you familiar with The Kola Peninsula in the Murmansk region?

"Yes, it's located in the northwestern part of Russia. It borders Finland and Norway. The Peninsula faces the Barents Sea in the north and the White Sea in the south," Oleg said proudly.

"Did you know that area of Russia has the greatest capacity for wind power in the world?"

"I did not know that. I know that another oil and gas field had been found under the seabed of the Barents Sea. The Shtockmonovskoye gas field is considered to be the largest offshore deposit of natural gas in the world."

"Really? That might be something that my group should look into. But this wind thing is the future, Oleg. The problem is that a lot of the area available for wind power in Russia is far from major cities. But right now there are settlements, fishing villages, border stations and shit like that, that are far from the electrical grid."

"Most of them are powered mainly by diesel generator sets."

"Right. So wind power will make a substantial contribution to the power supply in these areas. And as the business capability and construction of new transmission lines moves forward, we can begin servicing some of the major cities."

"You sound just like a businessman, my friend."

"Too much, Oleg," Black said and wondered if he was a legitimate businessman playing gangster or a gangster playing legitimate businessman. "What do you think, Oleg? You ready to make some real money? 'Cause I'm sure that this will be far more lucrative for you than Ms. West's little pussy business."

"Yes, yes, I can see where that would be much more lucrative—long term of course."

"Of course."

Oleg held out his hand. "I think we have an under-standing."

"I'm glad to hear that," Black said and shook Oleg's hand. All he had to do now was convince Martin Mar-shall and his Chinese partners that involving Oleg and the Izmaylovskaya mob was a good idea.

Oleg poured another round of drinks. "Come. We drink to our new partnership. To you, Mikhail."

"And to you, Oleg, but tell me something."

"What is that?"

"You said when Angelo called you that you had your suspicions about the reason I wanted to talk to you. What did you mean by that?"

"I have heard from some associates that you have big problems. That is what I thought you wanted to talk to me about."

"What kind of problems are we talking about?"

"Come," Oleg said and stood up. "We continue this conversation outside."

Black stood up and so did Victor.

"No," Oleg said. "We talk alone," Oleg said and Black followed him out the back door. The two men walked down the alley and out into the street before Oleg spoke. "One of your men was killed recently."

"Yes," Black said and looked at Oleg curiously. "But now I'm wondering why you would think I would want to talk to you about that. Unless you're tellin' me that you or your associates had something to do with it."

"No, no, I assure you that we had nothing to do with your man's death, but as I said, I do hear things."

"What kind of things?"

Oleg took out a pack of cigarettes and offered Black one. When he refused, Oleg lit up and continued. "Are you familiar with a man named Cruz Villanueva?"

"Yes, Oleg. I'm very familiar with Mr. Villanueva."

"I hear that he is planning to make a move uptown?"

"I heard that, too."

"There are things going on in your organization, Mikhail. And it is more than just your man getting killed and Cruz planning to move uptown, although they are connected."

"Are you telling me that Cruz had him killed?"

"This I do not know. But what I can tell you, Mikhail, is that someone in your organization is doing business with my associates without your knowledge."

"Bo."

"I do not know what his name is, Mikhail," Oleg said and stopped walking. He turned to Black and put his hand on his shoulders. "I can only tell you that this man, he talks a lot about the way things will be once you are gone and he is in charge."

CHAPTER TWENTY-SEVEN

Black walked back to the restaurant with Oleg and thanked him for the information. "Where's Bo?" he asked Victor as soon as they were back in the car. Once Black explained to Victor what Oleg had told him, Victor called Sabrina. As was their custom, he let the phone ring once and ended the call. Five minutes later, Sabrina called him back. She said that she didn't know where Bo was and that he'd left earlier with Hank, and she hadn't seen or heard from him since. Black told Victor to tell Sabrina that if she saw or heard from Bo that she could call him, and then get the fuck away from Bo.

"Where to now?" Victor asked as he drove back to the Bronx.

"Let's go find Cruz," Black said. "And let me see your phone." Black tried Bobby's cell again, and once again, it went straight to voicemail. Then he tried him again at the club before calling Nick on his cell phone.

"Nick, its Black. Where are you?"

"Me and Bobby are on our way to take care of something," Nick said.

"There are some things goin' on that I need to talk to you two about. When you get done, y'all meet me at Cynt's."

"We'll meet you there when we're done. We got some things that we need to let you know about."

"Am I gonna be happy about it?"

Nick looked at Bobby. "He wants to know if he's gonna be happy about what we did," he said and handed Bobby the phone.

"What's up, Mike? No, you're not gonna be happy about it, but trust me, what me and Nick are doin' tonight has to be done. Where you at?"

"Me and Victor are about to take care of something, so I'll see you two later at Cynt's," Black said and ended the call.

Black and Victor headed back to the Bronx and checked out the spots where they thought they might find Cruz until they got word that he was at his apartment.

When Black and Victor arrived at Cruz's they got out and headed for the building. As soon as they got close to it, somebody began shooting at them. Both Black and Victor took out their guns and ran toward the building, firing shots as they ran until they made it to the building.

"Think that was meant for us?" Victor asked while he reloaded his weapon.

"Let's go find out," Black said and went inside.

They got on the elevator and Black pressed the button for the fourth floor. "But Cruz is on six."

"Stick with me, kid, and learn something," Black said as the door closed. "Right now there's at least two, maybe three mutha fuckas standing in front of the door. When the door opens on six they're gonna start shooting. Do you really wanna be in here when that happens?"

"Not really," Victor replied and felt a little stupid.

The elevator stopped on the fourth floor and they stepped to either side as the door opened. Black stuck his head out of the elevator and looked in both directions. The hallway was clear. Black pressed the button for the sixth floor. "Come on."

They ran to the stairwell and made their way up the steps. When they got to the fifth floor they heard gunfire. "You were right," Victor said and continued up the steps behind Black.

"Stick with me, kid, and you just might learn a few things and live long enough to use them," Black said as he got to the door. "You ready?"

"Let's do it."

Black opened the door, stuck his gun out and fired blindly down the hall before he stepped out. There were two men with their backs to the wall. They opened fire and started backing their way down the hall toward Cruz's apartment. Victor began firing shots from the doorway. Black hit the floor and fired at the men. He shot one in the back as he turned to run. Victor hit the other with two shots to the chest to clear the hallway.

Black got up and started walking down the hall. Just then, Jorge stuck his head out of the apartment and began firing. Black rammed his shoulder into the door of another apartment and took cover inside. Both Black and Victor began firing at Jorge from their positions.

While Jorge covered for him, Cruz came running out of the apartment and down the hall.

"There he goes," Black shouted and went after Cruz. Jorge ducked back in the apartment. Victor reloaded his weapon then came out of the stairwell and started down the hall.

As Black passed by the apartment Jorge came out the door and prepared to fire. "Behind you, Black," Victor yelled and took aim.

Black turned in time to see Victor drop Jorge with a shot to the head. He nodded his appreciation at Victor and went after Cruz.

When Black got to the stairwell, he could see Cruz running down the steps two floors below. He fired a couple of shots and went after him. On the way down the steps, Black changed the clips in his guns.

When Cruz got to the first floor he stopped and fired a shot at Black. He fired back and hit Cruz in the leg. Cruz took a couple more shots and continued down the steps into the basement.

Black followed him in.

When he entered the basement was dark. There were only two lights in the distance. It was obvious from the cobwebs that very few people went down there. As he searched the basement for Cruz, Black could hear what sounded like rats moving across the floor.

Black moved slowly toward the light with both guns drawn until his foot hit a beer can. Cruz heard the sound and fired in that direction, but it wasn't close. Black picked up the can and threw it. When the can hit the floor Cruz fired again. Black saw where the shot came from and moved carefully toward it.

As Black came to a clearing he found Cruz sitting on the floor in a corner. Cruz raised his weapon and pulled the trigger, but he was out of bullets.

"Hello, Cruz."

Cruz threw the gun at Black, but he stepped out of the way. He picked up the empty gun and hit Cruz in the face with it. Black could see the blood pooling around his leg. He stepped on the wound and put his weight on it.

"Ouchhh, shit!" Cruz yelled in pain.

Black knelt down next to Cruz. "Was all this really necessary? I only wanted to talk."

"Fuck you, Black."

Black hit Cruz in the face with the barrel of his gun. "Doesn't matter now."

"You gonna kill me anyway," Cruz said.

"You're right. You're gonna die. But before I kill you, I'm curious. Why'd you start shooting at me when we got out the car?"

Cruz didn't answer so Black shot him in the other leg. Then he pressed the barrel into the wound.

"Okay, okay, shit. Man said you was comin' to get me for killin' Kenny. But I told you, I ain't have nothing to do with that shit."

"Then tell me who did?"

"Fuck you, man. I ain't no fuckin' snitch. Go ahead and fuckin' shoot. I die like a fuckin' man."

Black looked around the darkened area and walked away without speaking. When he came back he had a chain in his hand. He swung the chain around, inching closer and closer to Cruz's face. Cruz didn't flinch and Black laughed. "You a tough mutha fucka."

He grabbed Cruz by the collar and dragged him to the open area of the basement. Then Black took the chain and tied Cruz to one of the support beams.

Black stood in front of Cruz and pointed his weapon and shot him once on the side of his stomach. Then he put the gun away and turned to leave.

"Where you goin'?" Cruz asked.

"I'm goin' to check on Victor. I left him upstairs to deal with your bitch Jorge. But I'll be back." Black took a few steps then he stopped and turned around. "Oh yeah. Watch out for the rats." Black started walking back toward Cruz slowly. "There's a lot of them down here. They're gonna smell that blood, and they're gonna come to feed. When they do, then we'll see just how tough a mutha fucka you really are," Black said and walked away.

"Black! Come back here, Black! Don't leave me down here. Black!" Cruz screamed.

Black could still hear him screaming until he closed the basement door and started up the steps. When he got to the third floor, Black could hear gunfire and he started to run up the steps. The gunfire had stopped by the time Black got to the sixth floor. He ran down the hall to the apartment. The door was open. Black set himself and went in. There were three dead bodies on the floor. Neither one of them was Victor. Black kicked over one of the bodies and saw that it was Jorge.

As he moved farther into the room, Black saw that there were drugs and money on the table. Black heard a noise and pointed his weapon in that direction.

"It's me, Black," Victor said quickly as he came out of one of the bedrooms with a suitcase in his hand.

Black looked around the room. "Not bad, kid. Not bad at all," he said as Victor moved to the table with the drugs and money. "Take the money, leave the rest."

"You want me to leave the dope?"

"What I just say?"

Victor looked at Black for a minute. "You're the boss."

When he had packed up all the money, Victor followed Black out of the apartment. They took the elevator down to the first floor. But instead of leaving the building, Victor was surprised when Black started walking down the hall toward the stairwell.

"Where we goin'?" he asked and followed Black to the basement door.

"Cruz is down here waitin' for me to come back."

Victor looked at Black curiously but followed anyway. As they opened the basement door, Victor could hear what sounded like somebody moaning in pain. The further into the basement they moved the louder the sound got. When they got to the open area of the basement, Black stopped and Victor said, "Oh shit."

Once they smelled blood, the rats moved in as Black had predicted and began to feed on the wounds on Cruz's legs and stomach.

Black fired one shot in Cruz's direction and the rats scattered. Black walked up and stood over Cruz.

"Who told you we were comin' for you?"

"It was Bo," Cruz said.

"Bo," Victor said.

"Bo said that you told him that even if I didn't have shit to do with killin' Kenny, I was a dead man."

"Who had Kenny killed?" Black asked.

"That was Bo too."

"Why?"

"He tried to get Kenny to turn on you. Bo wanted him with us when we took on Stark. When he wouldn't flip, Bo had to kill him," Cruz said.

"Thank you," Black said and shot Cruz twice in the head.

Victor looked back at Cruz as they walked away. By the time they got to the steps, the rats had returned to their meal. Black and Victor returned to the car and put the suitcase with the money in the truck.

Once they were in the car, Black turned to Victor. "Let me see your phone." Black dialed a number.

"Hello."

"Monika, its Black."

"What's up?"

"Meet me at Cuisine in twenty minutes. I got something I need you to take care of tonight."

"See you there," Monika said and hung up.

CHAPTER TWENTY-EIGHT

The first person Rain saw when she got to JR's was Rose. She was the manager of the club. The police were still there and Rain didn't want to talk to them until she got with Rose first. She grabbed Rose by the arm and practically dragged her to the office.

"What happened?" Rain asked as soon as the door was closed.

"Like I told you when I called, five masked men came through the back door with guns."

"Where was security? Who was on the door?"

"Keith was on the door like he usually is."

"And he just let five masked mutha fuckas with guns in?"

"He said when he looked at the monitor there was an employee at the door."

"Who?"

"He didn't say. He said he buzzed them in and before he knew it, they were in and had hit him in the head with something."

"Where is he now? I wanna talk to him."

"He was bleeding pretty bad. The paramedics took him to the hospital."

"All right, I'll deal with him later. What happened then?" Rain went to the bar and picked up a bottle.

"They fired a couple of shots and everybody got out of the way. Then two of them went for the safe in the office and the other three went straight for the gambling room."

"Where were you?"

"In the office," Rose said quietly.

"You opened the safe for them, didn't you?"

Rose dropped her head. "Yes." Then she looked at Rain. "I'm sorry, Rain, but they had a gun to my head. I thought they were gonna kill me."

"Don't sweat it, Rose. You did the right thing," Rain said and poured them both a drink. "Who called the cops?"

"I swear 'for God, Rain, I don't know. I was down in the gambling room when Ronnette came and told me the cops were here. I had her to hurry up and get the people out of there, and change the room over."

One of the things her father did was, he left a lot of boxes, old tables and chairs, and bar supplies up against the walls all around the gambling room. When Rose found out the cops were in the club, knowing that it wouldn't take them long to make their way down there, she got the men to cover the gambling equipment with the stuff around the walls, so the room looked like it was nothing but storage.

"You did good, Rose," Rain told her.

"I need to get back out on the floor," Rose said and got up.

"Hey, Rose," Rain said before Rose walked out of the office.

"Yes."

"Where was Blue while all this was goin' on?"

"I haven't seen him all night."

"Okay. You can go."

While Rain was gathering information about the robbery, detectives Kirk and Richards were on their way to JR's to talk to her. They had read over her arrest record and were not impressed. "I don't know about you, Pat, but I'm not seeing this," Kirk said.

"What do you mean?"

"Look at this. She's got a couple of arrests for possession of less than an ounce of blow and a gun charge. This doesn't say drug kingpin to me. I just don't think that this little girl, and that's what she is, she's only twenty-three, is the one we're looking for."

"They grow up fast these days. But I see your point. I'm more incline to agree with Sanchez on this one. Rain Robinson is small time," Richards concluded.

"She still may be able to give us something about this Rockwell character, but her being PR, no, Pat, I'm not buying it," Kirk said as his cell phone rang and he was told about the robbery at JR's. "I may have spoken too soon."

"What do you mean?"

"Her club, JR's, it just got robbed."

"Really?"

"Really. So if she is PR, robbing the club may just be a part of somebody's plan to take her down."

"This keeps getting better all the time," Richards commented and drove a little faster.

Rain sat alone in her office at JR's thinking. How did things fall apart so fast? She only had one dope spot that was still up and running. Other than the product she took from Rockwell's, Rain was out of product and out of money. She wasn't sure how much money they took from the gambling spot, but there was thirty grand in the safe.

She knew that Nick would take care of the gambling. He would bring in his own people and beef up security. Something she should have done a long time ago, or at the very least when Nick mentioned that he thought security was a little lax. But when she told Blue Claxton about it, he said that this was how they had run their security for years, and he saw no reason to change it just because Nick said so.

Never having had much involvement in the gambling operation when her father was alive, Rain took his word for it. Now she had paid the price for her stubborn ignorance. One thing was certain; Nick wouldn't be refinancing her drug operation. The long and short of it was Rain was out of business.

She was mad at Nick. In her eyes, he had run out on her. One thought rolled around in her mind. *What could he possibly have to do that was more important than comin' with me to check on our spot?*

And it was their spot. Sure the club was hers, but they were partners in the gambling. Rain could only think of one thing, one reason that Nick would leave her at a time like that.

That uppity-bitch Wanda.

She had gotten tired of Nick leaving her to go be with Wanda. She was glad that it was over between them. Rain was determined to make sure they stayed over. Nick was her man now and hers alone.

Rain had to put that anger behind her and handle her business. Then she thought, *Maybe Nick is testin' me. Seein' how I handle shit like this.*

Rain always believed that she could do more to help Nick run his show. Maybe this was her opportunity to step up. One thing stood in the way of that. Rain knew how Nick, and Black for that matter, felt about drugs.

Maybe me being out of business is a good thing. Now that I got Nick all to myself, I need to get with the program and put the dope game behind me.

Rain thought about what Jay Easy said to her before she killed him. "Go ahead and do it. But even if you kill me the shit won't stop. It will only get worse. You got more enemies than just me."

Who were her enemies and how many were there? Why were they doing this to her? What would they hit next? Rain didn't have to wait long for the answer to one of her questions.

The phone rang.

"This Rain."

"Rain, this is Rodney C at the warehouse. We just got robbed."

"Fuck!" Rain yelled. "What happened?"

"There were five of them. They came down in the elevator, killed Bennie, Howard, Marvin and three other people."

"Who the fuck is Bennie?"

"The elevator man. They killed him first. When the elevator doors opened, Howard and Marvin started shootin'. But they was out-gunned."

"What about the other people?"

"Got hit by stray bullets."

"Cops there?"

"Nah."

"What about the bodies?"

"We takin' care of that."

"Where is Blue?"

"He ain't been here all night."

"You ain't seen him, huh?"

"Nope. I been runnin' things."

"You know we got hit over here too?"

"For real?"

"So if you see that mutha fucka Blue, you call me and keep him there 'til I get there. You hear me?"

"You got it." Rodney C said and Rain slammed the phone down. Hearing that Blue Claxton hadn't been to either spot all night made her think that he had to be involved.

Blue knew enough about both operations to pull it off and he was always beefin' with her about letting Nick take over. "Got to be that nigga," Rain said and picked up the phone. She called Nick, but he didn't answer.

When Rain called Nick, he and Bobby were in the car on their way to JR's to deal with her.

"That her?" Bobby asked as Nick looked at his phone, but didn't answer.

"Yeah," Nick said quietly.

"She'll call back."

"No she won't."

"If she does, find out where she is and get her to meet you some place," Bobby recommended. "Some place secluded. We don't need no crowd."

"This ain't my first time, Bobby," Nick said.

Bobby looked over at him. "You want me to do it?"

"No. This is my problem, I need to handle it myself," Nick said, but it was obvious to Bobby that he didn't want to be the one to do it.

"You know this is what we gotta do, right?" Bobby asked. "If we don't, she'll end up takin' all of us down with her."

"I know."

When Nick didn't answer her call, Rain was furious. She threw her cell phone across the room. She went to the bar and poured herself a shot of Patrón. Rain drank it down, and got a different gun from the safe. Then she went to pick up her phone and left the office.

She made her way through the crowded club. If she didn't know that there had been a robbery, she couldn't tell it by the crowd. Rain wandered around the club until she found Rose. "Rose! You see Blue you, call me."

"Okay."

"Make sure he don't leave."

"Where you goin'?"

"To the warehouse. They got robbed too," Rain said and walked away.

When she got outside and headed for her car, she saw Blue getting out of his car. Her anger welled up inside her as she walked toward him. Rain wanted to pull her pistol and blast him as soon as she got close enough, but there were too many people around.

Instead of getting him someplace where they could talk quietly and there were less witnesses, Rain confronted him as soon as she was close enough to do so.

"Where you been all fuckin' night, nigga?"

"I had some shit to do," Blue said.

"You know I got hit tonight? Of course you do, 'cause your ass was in on it."

"What is you sayin'?"

"I know it was you, Blue."

"You're crazy. Fuckin' wit' that nigga done made you stupid."

"I'm smart enough to finally see your bitch-ass for what you really are: a lyin'-ass backstabbin' bitch!"

While Rain and Blue were arguing they didn't notice that Kirk and Richards had arrived at JR's and were checking out Rain's car.

"Gray Taurus," Richards pointed out as they passed.

"We come to the right place," Kirk said as they got closer to the club.

At that moment, Bobby and Nick arrived at JR's and got out of the car. "There she is," Nick said, "arguin' with Blue."

"Get her away from that nigga and let's get this over with. Ain't that Kirk and Richards," Bobby noticed.

"Shit! That's all we fuckin' need," Nick said.

"He don't need to see us," Bobby said, and he and Nick stood by the car.

The argument raged on.

"You are stupid. Too stupid to know who your real friends are!" Blue shouted.

"Real friends like Jay Easy," Rain said and Blue went silent. "Yeah, that's right, Jay Easy. That nigga told me everything right before I put a bullet in his brain. All I wanna know is why?"

"Because the shit you been doin' just ain't right!" Blue yelled and got in Rain's face.

"What is you talking about?"

"You givin' up everything Jeff Ritchie and your daddy built to Nick. And turnin' your back on Jay Easy for that nigga was wrong."

"So you backed Jay Easy's play?"

Blue laughed at Rain. "You are a fool, Rain. A fuckin' fool who don't know shit 'bout what's really happening."

"What you talkin' about?"

"One of Nick's people was behind Jay Easy."

"Who?"

"Bo Freeman was backin' Jay Easy."

"You know what, fuck this." Rain started to pull out her gun, but Blue was faster with his and shot Rain in the chest.

"Police—freeze!" Richards yelled with his gun drawn.

"Drop the gun!" Kirk yelled.

Blue turned and pointed his gun in the direction of the two detectives and fired. Kirk returned fire and hit Blue with several shots.

Nick saw Rain lying on the ground and started to go to her, but Bobby held him back. "Let her die."

Nick jerked away from Bobby and turned away.

"Come on, lets get outta here before Kirk sees us," Bobby said, and he and Nick got in the car.

CHAPTER TWENTY-NINE

It was quiet at Clay's garage. The only people there were Bo and Hank. The phone rang and Bo answered it. While Hank looked on, Bo listened and nodded his head. Then a smile came across his face. Bo hung up the phone and pulled a bottle of Glenlivet 12 Year Single Malt Scotch Whisky out of the desk drawer and two paper cups.

"What's the occasion?" Hank asked as Bo poured the liquor.

"We celebratin'."

"What we celebratin'?"

"That was Bull Harris on the phone. He just heard that the cops found Stark and Moon dead at Fat Larry's. I'm bettin' that it was Nick who killed them."

"It's begun," Hank said and turned up his drink.

"Damn right, it's begun. It's better than that. He said that Blue Claxton shot Rain outside of JR's."

"Where's Blue now?"

"Dead."

"Dead?"

"Stupid mutha fucka shot that bitch in front of the cops, and they smoked his ass."

Hank laughed and refilled his drink. "That's fucked up."

"For who? Shit is fucked up for that nigga, maybe. But the shit's workin' out perfect for us. Shit, we was gonna have to kill that nigga and that dumb-ass cry baby Jay Easy anyway."

"That nigga was pathetic. Cryin' like a fuckin' girl over that bitch," Hank laughed. "'Rain left me for that nigga. She hurt me, hurt me bad'," Hank said, imitating Jay Easy.

"I wanted to put a bullet in that nigga's brain right then," Bo said laughing.

"If you had, we wouldn'ta made all that money sellin' all that caine he stole from Rain to Cruz," Hank said.

"You know, Hank, shit is workin' out better than I planned." Bo walked to the door of his office and looked out into the garage.

"With Stark, Moon and Rain dead, sooner or later Black is gonna find out that Stark was supplyin' Rain."

Bo spun around quickly. "What you mean sooner or later? I'ma tell him myself in the mornin' at Kenny's funeral," Bo laughed. "See, I had the shit figured right from the jump. When I found out that Stark was supplyin' Rain, I knew for a fact that once Nick found out about it, he would kill Stark; if for no other reason than to keep that shit from Black. That nigga would lose his mind if he found that shit out."

"Yeah, bad enough Nick was fuckin' around with Rain on Wanda. Shit, Freeze told me that Black said he would kill Nick over Wanda. But if Black found out that the bitch was dealin', shit," Hank said.

"Black would kill her and Nick."

"I heard how Black did Banks when he found out that nigga was dealin'."

"Shit, Nick and Freeze beat the shit outta him then they burnt the nigga with acid, before Black said the nigga was guilty of treason, put a bag over his head and shot him."

"Them niggas didn't play in those days."

"That was then. Now them niggas soft as paper. Tryin' to go legit, shiiit. Let Wanda's bitch-ass blow that smoke up they ass."

"I don't know about all that now. It wasn't soft how Black dealt with the three young niggas that tried to kill him and Bobby in that drive-by. And what about Mylo and that other DEA agent?"

"How long ago was that? Since then, them niggas been laid back gettin' soft. Back in the day, Black would never get involved with a nigga like Stark. I don't give a fuck what that pussy-ass Angelo wanted. Back in the day, Black woulda shot that cracker in the head for sayin' something like that to him. Now, that nigga rolled over and got in bed with them mutha fuckas to keep the peace."

"Well, either way, Bo, you had the shit figured. Only thing you didn't figure right was Kenny," Hank said.

"Yeah." Bo dropped his head. "I just knew he'd be down for it. I thought that since Kenny didn't like Nick, he would back me in this shit." Bo had planned to kill Nick since the day Black came to the garage and told him that he had picked Nick to takeover for Freeze, over him.

"But you was wrong there."

"Kenny knew Freeze dying was Nick's fault, but what I didn't count on was Kenny being so loyal to Black. When he said that shit to me I had to kill him."

"Told you that nigga wasn't ever gonna turn on Black. They go too far back."

"But, fuck it now, shit's done."

"You oughta call Cruz. Tell him the good news."

Bo walked back to his desk and picked up the phone. "Now that Stark is dead, Cruz can make his move." He sat down and dialed a number. Cruz was a big part of Bo's plan. He had promised Cruz control of Stark's market once he was dead.

Once again, Hank looked on while Bo held the phone and listened. Only this time he wasn't smiling.

Bo hung up the phone and poured himself another drink and shot it quick.

"What's wrong?"

"That was Cruz's old lady, Sonya. She said Cruz and Jorge are dead."

"What?"

"She said just got home and she found Jorge and four of their boys dead; two in the hallway and Jorge and two others in the apartment. And they found Cruz in the basement. He was chained to a pole, shot in head. She said the rats was eatin' his ass when they got there."

"Black," was all Hank had to say.

"You think Black did that shit?" Bo asked.

"I wouldn't bet against it. I mean, think about that shit. Stark was supplyin' Rain. You had everybody believin' that Cruz killed Kenny 'cause he wanted Kenny with him on his move uptown. Now on the same night they both turn up dead. On the same fuckin' night!" Hank shouted. "I'm tellin' you Black behind that shit."

Bo dropped his head in his hands. "It do sound like some shit Black would do."

"That nigga cleanin' house, Bo."

"If Black did kill Cruz, all I gotta do is kill Nick and I'd control it all."

"What make you so sure that if Nick was dead Black would turn to you?"

"Who else would Black turn to?"

"Suppose Cruz told him that you had Kenny killed and you planned to kill Nick?"

"You're right. I have to kill Black."

"And that means you gotta kill Bobby."

"I need to take the three of them out at once." Bo picked up the phone again and made a call to set it up. "Put the word out. Kill Black, Bobby and Nick on sight."

Bo hung up the phone and poured him and Hank another drink. "You did what you had to do at this point, Bo."

"Yeah," Bo said, but he still felt bad about it. He respected Black on so many levels. He never wanted to kill Black, just Nick. Now he had given the order to kill Black on sight.

Bo finished his drink and stood up. "I'm about to get outta here. Kenny's funeral is tomorrow. The least I could do is pay my respects to that nigga."

"You go ahead. I'll close up here." Hank said.

"See you tomorrow," Bo said and walked out of the office. He made his way through the garage to the door.

Bo stopped at the door and looked around. Soon all this would be behind him, and he would be in control of

Black's organization. A smile came across his face and he walked out of the garage to his car.

Bo got in his car and closed the door. When he put the key in the ignition and turned it, the car exploded.

Inside the garage, Hank heard the explosion and ran outside to see what happened. When Hank got to the door he saw Bo's car in flames. "Bo," he called out, but Bo was dead, and he knew it.

Hank assumed that he was right. Cruz must have told Black that Bo was behind it all, and Black took care of him. And if that was the case, Hank knew that he was next. He had to get out of the city right away.

Hank shook his head and started to approach the burning car. He was only able to take a couple of steps before Hank was shot twice in the chest.

With her job completed, Monika broke down her sniper's rifle and left the scene.

CHAPTER THIRTY

Monika drove away from Clay's Garage and pulled out her cell phone to make her report. "Black still with you?" she asked Victor.

"Hold on," he said and handed Black the phone.

"What's up?"

"It's done," she said.

"How'd he go?" Black asked his assassin.

Monika laughed. "Up in smoke."

"What about the other one?"

"He took two, but he's gone, too."

"Any problem?"

"Are there ever?"

"You're the woman. We'll talk in the morning." Black thought for a second. "You *are* going to come to Kenny's funeral, aren't you?"

"I hadn't planned on it," Monika said.

"Under the circumstances, I'd appreciate it if you did."

"Understood. I guess I'll see you in the morning. "

"Monika."

"Yeah."

"Come heavy," Black said, letting Monika know that he wanted her to come armed to the funeral.

"Is there any other way with me," Monika said, reminding Black that she was always armed.

Black laughed a little. "That's why I love you, big ass."

"You keep on talkin' that shit and one day I'm gonna hold a gun to your head and take me some of that big dick."

"Promises, promises," Black said and ended the call. He handed the phone back to Victor. "Take me by Cynt's and then you can go fuck Sabrina."

"What about Bo?" Victor asked as he drove toward Cynt's.

"Oh yeah, I forgot to tell you, Bo is dead. His car blew up."

"Hank?"

"Hank took two. He's dead too."

"Mind if I ask you a question."

"Go ahead."

"Who is Monika?"

"She does things for me. You'll meet her tomorrow."

Victor parked Black's Cadillac in front of Cynt's and handed the keys to Black. "You did good tonight, kid."

"Thanks for lettin' me ride with you. I know I can learn a lot from you," Victor said.

Black threw him back the keys to the Caddy. "You know where I live?"

"Yes, sir," Victor said.

"The funeral is at eleven. Pick me up at ten thirty."

"What about the money in the trunk?"

"You keep it," Black said and walked away. "And don't be late," he shouted as he went inside of Cynt's.

227

The place was closed when Black went inside. Not even Cynt, who was always there long after they closed, was there. Black turned on a few lights and headed for the bar.

He went behind the bar and poured himself a glass of Rémy. Black stood behind the bar and thought about what had gone on that night, and how it changed things in his world.

All of a sudden Bo and Hank were dead, Oleg was his new partner, and then there was Jada West. Black took a sip of his drink. "What to do with Jada West?" he asked himself.

If he wanted to be honest about it, Black liked Jada on more than just a business level. Liked her style and the way she carried herself. He thought she was beautiful since the first time he saw her dance. That night, and every time they met since, he could feel the energy between them.

Black poured himself another drink and thought about what he should do with Jada West and her skill set; training women to be high-price hookers. He thought about his expansion into the gambling market in Nassau and the clientele that Jamaica had begun to attract to his spots. Then he remembered something that Jamaica said to him one night. "All we need now is some girls, and we take all their money."

At the time, Black didn't think that the international tourist clientele the island attracted would be willing to pay for the caliber of women that currently worked the trade in Nassau. However, if Jada West could recruit and train high-quality talent from around the world,

Black was sure that there was definitely a market for that.

Just then, Bobby and Nick came in and approached the bar. "Okay, so tell me what I'm not going to be happy about," Black said and got two more glasses.

"Hello, Mike. How you doin' tonight?" Bobby asked.

"I'm good," Black said and pushed a glass of Rémy at Bobby, and then poured a glass of Johnny Walker Black for Nick. He left both bottles on the bar. "Now tell me what you two did that I'm not gonna be happy about."

"Thanks for the drink," Bobby said and raised his glass. Then he turned to Nick. "Tell him."

"Me?" Nick said and took a big shallow of his drink. "I needed that. But why do I have to be the one?"

"This was your show from the start," Bobby said and walked away from the bar. He sat down at a table close to the bar.

"One of you needs to tell me right now."

"Bobby killed Stark and Moon tonight," Nick said and finished his drink.

"You killed Moon," Bobby said quickly.

"What did you say?"

"Bobby killed—"

"I heard what you said, Bobby!" Black yelled. "Why the fuck did you kill Stark?"

Bobby got up and went to the bar. "Nick—" was all he said then poured himself another shot of Rémy.

"Rain was dealin' and Stark was supplyin' her."

"So you killed him and Moon for that? That's a reason to make him stop, not kill him."

Bobby smiled. "Nick—" was all he had to say.

"Her dealers were gettin' robbed and executed," Nick said.

"Tell him the rest," Bobby said.

"Kirk was on the case, and—" Nick said.

"Wait a minute. PR?" Black asked.

Nick and Bobby both nodded their heads.

"Purple fuckin' Rain?" Black asked in disbelief.

Nick and Bobby both nodded their heads.

"You gotta be kiddin' me," Black said.

"When Nick told me about it, I remembered Kirk comin' by Cuisine and askin' us about PR," Bobby said. "He had already been to see Stark. It was only a matter of time before Kirk put it all together and connected Rain to Nick and then we'd be fucked. It was time to clean up loose ends, and I started with Stark."

"What did you two do to Rain?"

"We were on our way to JR's to take care of her, but when we got there Blue shot her," Bobby explained.

"Why did Blue shoot her?"

"I don't know," Nick said quietly and sat down at a table.

"What happened to Blue?"

"Kirk shot him," Nick said.

"What the fuck was Kirk doin' there—never mind, he probably connected Rain to the robberies. You did the right thing, Bobby."

"Yeah, I know," Bobby said and joined Nick at the table. "How was your night?" he asked.

"My night was interesting. I found out why Kenny was killed and who was behind it."

"You gonna keep us in suspense?" Bobby asked.

Just then, four men burst into Cynt's firing automatic weapons. Black grabbed his gun and fired back while Nick and Bobby turned over the table they were sitting at and took cover.

The gunmen spread out and positioned themselves around the room and continued firing. While Nick and Bobby fired back, Black pushed a button under the bar. It opened a panel that led to a safe stocked with weapons. Black opened the safe and took out two semi-auto weapons and some clips.

Black loaded the weapons and stood up. He began firing at the gunmen as they moved closer to the bar. He hit one of the gunmen with multiple shots.

"Nick," Black yelled and threw him a weapon before taking cover behind the bar, as the remaining three gunmen fired at him.

Now it was Nick that came up firing, which gave Bobby enough cover to get behind the bar. When Black saw Bobby come behind the bar and going for the safe, he moved to the other end to get a better angle at the shooters.

Nick continued firing and shot the second gunmen. Bobby jumped over the bar armed with two forty-fives and took cover behind the overturned tables. He came up firing.

Black came out from behind the bar and was able to get behind one of the gunmen. With one shot he took out the third gunmen.

The forth gunmen fired shots wildly as he tried to make it to the door and out of Cynt's. When he turned to run, Bobby went after him. When he turned to fire,

Bobby walked toward him shooting with both guns. He went down hard.

"Everybody all right?" Black asked.

"I'm all right," Nick said and looked at Bobby. He stood over the man he'd just shot. The man moved and Bobby put two in his head. "I think he's dead, Bobby."

"Just makin' sure," Bobby said and reloaded his weapon.

"Nick, check outside and make sure there's nobody else out there," Black ordered.

"I'll go with him," Bobby said and followed Nick to the door. Once he had a look around, Nick came back inside. "All clear out there, Black."

"Anybody recognize anybody?" Bobby asked and looked at one of the dead gunmen.

"I do," Nick said. "These two are Bo's people."

"Bo," Black said. "It figures. He arranged the hit on Kenny. I thought he just wanted to kill you, Nick, but this boy was more ambitious than I gave him credit for. Mutha fucka wanted us all dead."

Bobby started walking toward the bar. "Let me get a drink, and then we go take care of that asshole."

"No need." Black joined Bobby at the bar. "Monika all ready took care of Bo and Hank."

CHAPTER THIRTY-ONE

The following morning, all gathered at Woodlawn Cemetery to pay their final respects to Kenny Lucas. Before the funeral began, Kirk and Richards arrived on the scene. There were a number of questions that the detectives needed answers to, and this was the best place to get them.

"See, Pat, they're all here."

"Yeah, but that don't mean we're gonna get anything out of any of them," Richards said as he and Kirk got out of their car and made their way toward the assembled guests.

"They are a tight-lipped bunch, always have been. But it's not always what they say, it's what they don't say and how they don't say it," Kirk claimed as the stood off to the side.

The minister spoke, "Love is the one virtue that goes on into eternity. Neither death nor time nor hell's fire could ever end true love. In sure and certain hope of the resurrection to eternal life through our Lord Jesus Christ, we commend to Almighty God our brother Kenny Lucas, and we commit his body to the ground, earth-to-earth, ashes-to-ashes, dust-to-dust. The Lord bless him and keep him. The Lord make his face to shine upon him and be gracious unto him and give him peace. Amen."

Once the service was over, the detective headed straight for Black, who was making his way back to his car along with CeCe and Victor.

"Good morning, detectives," Black said as soon as they were close enough to hear him. "I'm surprised to see you gentlemen, but I appreciate you coming to pay your respects."

"Whatever," was Detective Richards' response.

"I was wondering if we could get a moment of your time, Black?" Kirk said, choosing to be a bit more diplomatic than his partner.

"Not a problem." Black turned to CeCe and Victor. "Would you two please excuse me while I talk to the detectives?"

"Sure," CeCe said and walked away to mingle with the other guests.

"I'll be right here if you need me, Black," Victor said.

"That won't be necessary. I'm sure I'll be safe with these two paragons of virtue," Black said as Victor stepped away. "So what can I do for you gentlemen?"

"You know me, Black; just a couple of questions. Maybe you could clear some things up for me," Kirk said and let out a little yawn. "Excuse me," the detective said as he covered his mouth.

"You look tired, detective."

"I had a busy night—double homicide. Some people you know."

"Who got murdered, detective?"

"Bruce Stark and Clifford Moon were found dead at Fat Larry's late last night."

"I hadn't heard that, detective," Black said.

"I'm surprised you hadn't heard about it. I heard you and him were close, Black."

"We talked about this, Kirk, remember? After that unfortunate business with him and The Commission, I wouldn't call us close."

"What about Lorraine Robinson?" Richards asked. "You know her?"

"She's Jasper Robinson's daughter, right?"

"That's her. After JR died, she took over his club."

"I haven't seen Lorraine since she was a little girl. Her and her brother Miles, were nice kids."

"Nice kids, huh?" Richards said. "She goes by the name Rain, and she turned out to be a drug dealer, and her brother is doing time for murder."

"You never know how kids are gonna turn out these days, do you?"

"I hear that her and Nick were really close," Richards pressed.

"You'd have to ask Nick about that, detective. He's around here somewhere," Black said to Richards and turned to Kirk. "But tell me; did something happen to Miss Robinson?"

"She was shot outside her club by a guy named Blue Claxton," Kirk explained. "Real shame. I was just about to question Miss Robinson on her involvement in several drug murders."

"You said she was shot, detective. Is Miss Robinson gonna live?"

"Doctors don't know if she's gonna make it or not. She's under guard in intensive care right now. She hasn't regained consciousness," Richards said.

"What about the guy that shot her?"

"He's dead."

"Then justice was served," Black said and started walking away from Kirk and Richards.

The detectives started walking right alongside him. "You know, Black, with all the talk about you, Collette, Stark and Nick being linked to Rain Robinson, I'm wondering if what I keep hearing is true."

"What's that, detective?"

"That you're getting back in the drug business."

"We talked about this, too, detective. But I'll say it again in case I wasn't clear the last time. I am definitely not even thinking about moving in that direction. So you can go home and get some rest."

"All the same, I'm watching you, Black," Kirk said, and he and Richards walked away.

After the detective left, Wanda walked up to Black. For the next few minutes Wanda talked about some issues with their legal businesses. "There is one more thing I need to tell you."

"What's that?"

"Nick and I aren't together anymore," Wanda said softly.

"What happened?"

"I'm sure you already know the reason why," Wanda paused. "I just got tired of people telling me about him and Rain Robinson."

"You ask Nick about it?"

"Of course I did, and naturally he denied it. You know how you men are. I just thought you should know."

"I'm sorry," Black said and hugged her.

Wanda saw CeCe watching them. "By the way, I'm having dinner with Marcus Douglas tonight. Wanna join me?"

"Marcus Douglas," Black said and thought for a second. "Ain't he the guy you were gonna get to defend me for killin' Cassandra?"

"That's him. He's moving to New York from Atlanta and opening a practice here."

"What brought that on?"

"He said that he needed a change, but he didn't really go into any details. I guess I'll find out tonight."

"I don't think so, Wanda. You two have a good time."

"That's the thing. It won't be just the two of us. He's bringing somebody with him. Somebody you know."

"Who's that?"

"Carmen Taylor."

"Carmen Taylor," Black said.

He hadn't thought about Carmen in years. Black had met her years ago on the train one day when he and Freeze were going to kill a Rasta named Desmond Kelly, who had been sent by Vincent Martin to kill him.

That day on the train Carmen told Black that she was a model and Black introduced her to a modeling agent named Calvin Cummings. That introduction was what started Carmen's career on the road to becoming a super model.

Carmen always had a thing for thugs, and she fell hard for Black. He was feeling her, too, but Black knew that Carmen had a future modeling. A future that would be better served if she didn't have, "A thug nigga like me in your life," Black told Carmen on their last night together. After that, Black avoided Carmen until she finally gave up and got serious about her career.

"What time?" Black asked.

"I'll send a car for you at six," Wanda said as CeCe walked up.

"I didn't mean to interrupt anything," CeCe said as Wanda passed her.

"You're not," Wanda said and frowned. "I was just leaving anyway. I'll see you tonight, Mike."

"I didn't mean to run her away," CeCe said.

"You didn't. She was leaving when you walked up. And besides, Wanda doesn't like you."

"Why not? She doesn't know anything about me. Or is it because she and your wife were close?"

"No. It took a long time before the two of them got on good terms."

"So why doesn't she like me?"

"I never asked. But you're more than welcome to ask her."

"Don't think I won't."

"But I don't think now is a good time."

"I'm not gonna step to her now, but I will at a more appropriate time. I never did anything to her for her not to like me," CeCe paused. "She ain't one of those bitches who expects everybody to kiss her ass, is she?"

"No, she's not like that. Wanda is just very protective of all of us; that's all."

"Protective of you, you mean. Your whole crew is, but I guess they have to be with a man in your position," CeCe said as Nick approached them.

"Got a minute?" Black asked.

"All the time in the world," Nick said.

Black turned to CeCe. "Would you excuse us for a minute?"

"Sure. I'm getting used to it," CeCe said and kissed him on the cheek.

Black watched CeCe as she walked away. Once CeCe was out of hearing range, he turned to Nick. "Kirk says that Rain is still alive. They got her in intensive care. Doctors don't know if she's gonna make it."

"He say anything else?"

"Bobby was right. Kirk put it together. He was about to question her about those drug murders. So what I need to know from you is, if Rain comes out of it, is she gonna stand up, or is she somebody we gotta worry about?"

"Rain won't talk," Nick said confidently. "I'm sure of that."

"For your sake I hope so."

"I want you to know that I'm sorry for letting things get so out of control with Rain."

"You should be. You shoulda known what she was doin'. Shit, I knew Rain was dealin'. I didn't know it was on that level or that she was buying from Stark. But you should have. I told you once before, you need to know everything that's goin' on in the organization you're runnin'. But you let that young pussy blind you to who Rain really was."

"You're right, I did." Nick started to walk away, but then he stopped. "Wanda told you about us?"

"What's up with that?"

"She was lookin' for me while I was tryin' to get on top of this thing with Rain. She wanted to know what I was doin' and who I was with. I know you didn't want Wanda

239

to know anything about your deal with Stark and Angelo, so—"

"So you kept your mouth shut and let Wanda believe what she wanted to believe."

"Which was the truth; I was fuckin' Rain and it cost me."

"I'd talk to her, but I don't think it would do much good at this point," Black told Nick and signaled for CeCe and Victor to come back. "I appreciate you takin' a hit like that. But losin' Wanda over Rain Robinson is the consequence of your actions. You just gotta man-up now and accept it," Black said as he opened the car door for CeCe.

Black and CeCe got in the back seat and Victor drove away. As they drove away, Black thought about Carmen Taylor.

ROY GLENN

END OF
COMMIT TO VIOLENCE

COMING IN 2010

KILLING THEM SOFTLY
An Erotic Tale of Murder

After his wife loses her baby and slips into a deep depression, Devin James becomes involved in an affair with Avonte Petrocelli, a married woman with issues of her own. Avonte recently found out that her rich husband has a new blonde mistress and wants a divorce. As the affair continues, they meet Qianna Patterson, an unstable woman fresh out of prison, with a history of violence.

The plan: murder Devin's wife for the insurance money. Once the deadly deed is done, their real intentions come to the forefront, and the murders and the drama begin.

Mike Black
Returns in
Beneath the Surface